ETTA

ETTA

A GIFTED CHRONICLES NOVELLA

AMANDA LYNN PETRIN

Get new release updates and exclusive content when you sign up to my mailing list.

For my family. All of you.

CHAPTER ONE

JANUARY 4TH, 1843

Cape Cod, Massachusetts

"Come on, littles ones, time for bed," I told my niece and nephew in as scary a voice as I could muster, chasing them down the hallway.

"Can you tell us a story?" Catherine asked, pouting her bottom lip so only a psychopath could deny her.

"Of course, my love. Which one do you want?" I covered them each with blankets, tucking the corners in so all you could see were their smiling faces and curly blond hair. They both took after their father's fair features, rather than my family's darker ones.

"The story about the French Princess?"

"Which one?" Billy asked. Most of my stories seemed to take place in Paris, and my niece loved princesses.

"One where they live happily ever after," she decided.

"What other stories are there?" I smiled, gently tapping her nose with my finger, getting giggles in return.

"Fun ones with knights and swords and magic," my nephew said excitedly.

"I think I have just the thing," I assured them before getting comfortable on the bed between them. I told the tale of Princesse Sophie locked up in a tower, forced to do chores for her evil step-mother until one day a knight showed up, battled a terrible swamp monster, and married the Princesse. "And they lived happily ever after," I told the sleeping forms on either side of me. I kissed their foreheads and found my heavily pregnant sister staring at me from the doorway.

"You are so good with them." Georgina gave me a hug once I got close, grateful I saved her from yet another bedtime adventure.

"They're wonderful kids," I said, following her to the sitting room.

"Most of the time," she agreed with a teasing smile. "When are you running off to Paris?" she asked, taking a seat in her rocking chair, rubbing her stomach in a consistent motion I don't even think she was aware of.

"I'll stay until the baby's born, and you're back on your feet."

"That's what you said after Billy," she reminded me.

"But then you had Catherine," I pointed out.

"And you said the same thing when I was pregnant with her."

"Yet again." I pointed to her stomach this time.

"Lorie, I appreciate your help more than anything, and I don't know what I would do without you, but someday I want to spoil your children the way you spoil mine. I don't want to be the reason you never left Massachusetts."

"Paris will still be there next year. I don't want to be the reason you went mad and put your children up for adoption," I teased. "I'm needed here."

"I won't argue the second part, but I will promise to ship them to you in Paris before I let anyone else have them."

"I appreciate that. If French men are anything like the ones here, I'll probably need the company."

"There you go, closing yourself off before you've even met them. Might as well just stay here forever," she sighed, her rubbing more targeted now.

"Another kick?" I asked.

"It's like he's trying to see if he can push his foot all the way through to the outside."

"You should get to bed then. Hopefully he'll sleep when you do," I urged, helping her to her feet.

"Someday you'll be the one who's the size of a house, and you'll see the baby never sleeps when you do," she argued.

"I look forward to it," I told her in complete honesty. Men either saw me as Georgina's little sister, or they didn't see me at all, but children loved me. The dream of having my own children was the only thing keeping me from staying here forever with my sister's family.

"You should get some sleep as well," she called, already on her way to her bedroom.

"I'll just bring Bruno in," I assured her. Our family dog was getting on in age and mostly blind, which meant he sometimes needed a little help finding his way indoors at night.

"Take my shawl," she decided, pointing to an emerald green fabric she had draped over a chair.

"Yes, mother," I teased, rolling my eyes. Our parents died seven years ago, when I was only fourteen, so I moved in with my big sister and her new husband. I've tried my best to return the favor with her little ones, but she was taking care of me long before she took me in.

"Bruno!" I called, going straight to the garden, where he usually got into the tomato plants. It was colder than I expected, so I pulled Georgina's shawl tighter around myself.

Bruno wasn't in the back, or the front of our property. I couldn't see anything in the darkness, but Bruno constantly made this very distinct wheezing noise that led me to worry how long he had left. He didn't usually wander off, but he would sometimes chase squirrels if they were loud enough, and always went after the neighbor's cat, who loved to antagonize him.

I went through our front gate and had just finished latching it when I felt a strong hand on my shoulder.

CHAPTER TWO

"Georgina," the voice said before realizing it was me. "You shouldn't be out this late on your own, Lorie" William warned. Relief flooded me as I recognized my brother-in-law. I could hear the drunkenness in his voice before I smelt the beer on his breath. He had taken to stopping by the tavern on his way home most nights, ever since Georgie got pregnant for a third time.

"Bruno wandered off again," I explained. I shivered, even with the shawl. I hadn't intended to be out this long, or I would have dressed more appropriately.

"That dog of yours is always getting lost," he shook his head, losing his balance in the process.

"Are you okay?" I moved closer to help him steady himself. It wasn't easy, considering he weighed twice as much as me, most of it muscle.

"I am now," he assured me. "Come to think of it, there was a dog in the alley over there. It didn't occur to me at the time, but he did kind of look like Bruno."

"I'll go check it out. Thank you."

I took a step away, to see if he could stand without my help, but he held on.

"I'll help you." He gave me a drunken smile. "You really shouldn't be on your own, and I'm not sure I could make it home without you."

I COULDN'T HELP but smile at his vulnerable honesty. He put his arm around me for stability, then guided me to an alley a few blocks away. I could hear a dog in the distance, but it sounded like a street mutt, not my old and weathered Bruno.

"I don't think he's here anymore," I said when we got to the end of the alley, checking behind a trash bin, the only hiding place I could see.

"No, I think we're alone."

Something in the way he said it sent a chill up my spine that had nothing to do with the weather.

"Let's get you home," I decided, trying to shake away the feeling and get us out of there. The streets had been just as empty on our way over, but the alley felt ominous. Dangerous even. Maybe it was time Bruno became an indoor dog.

"I think we've got a little time." William smiled like he saw nothing wrong with the dark alley. I could hear the noise from the tavern in the distance, but there was nothing more than back doors to closed shops around us.

"It's getting cold and I have an early morning," I argued.

"Taking care of your sister's children because she keeps getting knocked up?"

He was drunk and didn't realize what he was saying, but this pent-up frustration after getting drunk with the guys was not a nice look on him.

"Don't you want someone to finally pay attention to poor, forgotten Loretta? Always in her sister's shadow, wanting things she'll never have."

"We should get you home," I repeated, more forcefully this time as I took his arm and tried to bring him out of the alley. It was no use taking his words personally when he was too drunk to remember any of them in the morning. Or so I told myself, but it stung.

"I said we had time," William stood his ground. He didn't sound drunk anymore. He sounded mean, as he grabbed my wrist with a lot more force than I could have mustered.

"Pretty shawl," he said, pulling it off my shoulders and bringing it to his cheek before letting it fall in a puddle.

It wasn't raining anymore, but there was a constant stream of water falling from a nearby roof. I hadn't heard it before, but the drip and my heartbeat were suddenly deafening, creating their own rhythm.

"Let's have some fun now, shall we?" William asked, pushing me back onto the brick wall and ripping the dress off my shoulders, tearing the fabric in the process.

"What are you doing?" I asked, horrified. I tried to pull the blue material back together, but I could see the white of my corset coming through.

"What do you think I'm doing?" He hiked up the folds of my skirt in case he hadn't made his intentions obvious.

"No," I argued, trying to push them back down. "You can't do this." I knew he was more upset than usual lately, but he had never acted as anything other than a protective older brother to me. The kind who would have murdered any man who even suggested he might do something like this to me.

"You'll find I can do whatever the hell I want, and no little bitch is going to stop me." His eyes were wild and terrifying as he played with his trousers, loosening the belt.

"I'll tell Georgina," I warned, feeling like a child, but the threat of telling my sister had always worked whenever kids from school would tease me. This wasn't quite the same situation, but it still stopped him.

"You won't," he spat. "You won't tell anyone about this."

"She'll know something happened," I argued.

"But she won't know it was with me. I heard there was a group of men preying on women who are out alone at night. It would be a shame if they fell upon you."

"William," I tried, hoping his name would somehow remind him who he was. Who I was to him.

"He's not here tonight," he said evenly. "All I see is a man with needs and a woman who better promise to keep her mouth shut." He looked at me, right into my eyes, and must have seen there was no way my sister wasn't finding out about this. Georgina felt like she had to protect me, ever since we were children. She would never forgive herself, or rest until he paid for this, whether he went through with it or not.

William's eyes changed at that moment. He no longer looked crazy; he was cold and emotionless. Determined.

"You don't want to do this," I pleaded, knowing it was useless as he took out his pocketknife. I couldn't reconcile what was happening with any form of logic.

His knife shimmered in the moonlight, making my heart constrict with fear.

"Please," I begged, but before I could argue my case, I felt something sharp slice into my stomach.

CHAPTER THREE

"Hello?" I heard a woman's voice coming from the street. It was so faint that I wasn't sure if I was imagining it.

William took the knife out of my stomach and buried it deep inside me again. Even if the woman was real, it wasn't like she could help me. I heard footsteps, but it sounded like she was running towards us instead of away from us. My brain was foggy, but I knew I had to warn her.

"Run," I yelled as loud as I could, but almost no sound came out as William stabbed me, yet again, this time leaving the knife inside me and looking in horror at what he'd done.

The woman showed up, with her brown curls flowing over her shoulders and wearing a white cloak that made her look like an angel. Especially when William got off of me and turned to her, back to his menacing stare. I tried to get up, to get her help, but my legs refused to move, and my arms were too weak to pull me. Even sitting up was making me dizzy.

There was a whir of movements, with him swinging a cane and her attacking him with her gloved hands, scratching at him as if she were a cat. Oddly enough, it seemed to be working.

William roared out in anger as they struggled over the cane, but the woman kneed him in the groin, so he doubled over.

"Run!" I tried again before he charged at her, pushing her into the brick wall he'd pushed me up against minutes before.

She did something to his arm that made him scream out in pain. He stared at her, and I was terrified of what he was going to do, but was not expecting it when he ran away from her, down the alley and into the street.

She chased after him, so I tried to drag myself to where I could call for help, clenching my jaw against the pain, but the alley was spinning and there was so much blood on the ground beside me.

I DIDN'T NOTICE the woman's return until she sat beside me, pressing her hands against my stomach to stop the blood, as I had done countless time while volunteering at the hospital, but I could tell from the look on her face that it wasn't working. She fished for something inside her purse and came out with a gun.

I would have jumped back in fear, but my body was too exhausted to resist. She might as well put me out of my misery rather than let me die alone in the alley.

I saw what looked like fireworks in the sky and understood that she had shot them up there rather than shooting me. It wasn't even seconds later that a man showed up, though I have no idea where he came from.

"What's wrong?" he asked, his voice full of worry, before he spotted me. He had a mess of dark hair that reminded me of my father, but I think he was my age, or Georgina's at the most.

"We need to help her," the woman said, with a fear in her voice that told me there was little she could do.

The man nodded before taking me up in his arms and carrying me through the empty streets, past the edge of town. I would have protested and asked him to bring me home, but every time I tried to say something, it came out as more of a whimper than words. I just needed to be back with Georgina, so she could take care of me and fix this, like she always did.

INSTEAD, the man carried me to a really big house by the water, going so fast it felt like I was on a horse. Or perhaps I drifted in and out of consciousness, because you couldn't get to the cape in less than an hour, unless you had a carriage. The entire area was unfamiliar to me, even though the trip seemed to last minutes at the most.

"She's lost a lot of blood." I could hear his voice, but it sounded distant.

"You're covered in it," a woman agreed, but I think she was different from the one who saved me; much older. I tried to open my eyes to see, but the lids were so heavy that all I could do was concentrate on her voice.

"Do you know what happened to her?" she asked. I placed her accent as Scottish, like she might have grown up there years ago, while the woman from earlier had definitely been American.

"Cassie found her. She's taking the carriage back." He placed me gently on what felt like a sofa by a fireplace, because it was soft and warm, whereas the ground had been cold and hard.

I could feel him pressing things to my stomach while she put cloths on my forehead, but the world disappeared and all I felt was cold, until I was woken by a door slamming and someone barging in.

"I told Delia we were done for the night," the woman from the alley told the man who was still applying pressure to my stomach. They'd called her Cassie. "How is she?"

"She has a pulse, but barely," the man told her. It was odd because I knew they were talking about me, but I felt entirely removed from the situation. I just wanted to go home. "What happened?" he asked.

"She was like this when I found her. There was a man, but he ran away."

"You didn't run after him?" he sounded surprised.

"She wasn't going to make it."

"She still isn't," he said sadly. I tried harder to lift my eyelids, to convince them not to give up on me.

The older woman brought blankets and someone tucked me in, like I'd done to the children earlier, but it didn't stop the cold that was taking over.

"I couldn't let her die alone in the street," Cassie explained her decision.

"It's okay," the man said, but it took me a moment to realize he was talking to me this time. I had finally managed to get my eyes open. His were as dark as his hair, but there was a softness to them. "I'm right here. I won't leave you. You're safe now," he told me.

I understood that he meant I was safe from whatever hurt me in the alley, but I wasn't actually going to be okay. Neither of them understood how not okay this was. No one was safe.

I tried to tell him, to use my last words to warn them about William, so they could know who did this to me, but my voice wasn't working.

"It's okay," he repeated, trying to calm me down.

I made one last attempt to get the words out, but it was like my body couldn't fight it anymore. My eyes closed and the world went dark. For a few seconds, I still heard his reassuring voice. Then I heard nothing at all.

CHAPTER FOUR

JANUARY 5TH, 1843

I woke up in a room I didn't recognize. It was sterile, like the hospital, only different. There were no windows, or even a mattress on the bed. It was colder somehow, and I wasn't wearing a gown. In fact, I wasn't wearing much of anything.

I was grateful for the small sheet that hardly covered my front, but definitely wasn't big enough to wrap around myself.

I crept into the next room and found a desk, some filing cabinets, and a large coat on top of the chair. Desperate times called for desperate measures, so I took the coat, put it on, and set off in search of someone who could tell me what was going on.

I was wandering the hallway when I heard a noise behind me. I didn't want to be discovered in such a state of undress, so I hurried to round the corner and crashed into a man in a white lab coat.

"I'm so sorry," I apologized, keeping my head down and gripping the coat shut. I could only imagine what I looked like. I hoped he wouldn't notice my lack of stockings...or shoes.

"No, I wasn't looking, I apologize."

"It's you," I realized. I looked up at the sound of his voice and found myself staring into those dark, intense eyes from last night.

"You're al...you're awake," he sounded much more surprised to see me than I was to see him.

"Why did you leave me in the morgue?" I asked, knowing that logically, that was where I woke up.

"My name is Gabriel, and the woman who found you last night was Cassandra—"

"What time is it?" I cut him off, realizing Georgina must be going crazy. I had promised to take Billy on an adventure this morning and patience was not his strong suit.

"Almost four," he shared.

"I have to get home before my sister wakes up. She'll be incredibly worried that I didn't come home."

"In the afternoon," he added. "I understand this is very confusing, but I think it's best if you come with me to Cassie's. She's just finishing an appointment upstairs, but we would be glad to fill you in and answer any questions."

I didn't have time to think before we heard footsteps coming down the hall. I was in no shape to meet people in an oversized men's coat and nothing else, so I followed him to the staircase. He waved his hand to the woman who saved me last night, before we quickly made our way to the back door.

"YOU MUST BE FREEZING," Cassie said when she followed me into the waiting carriage, handing me a large wool blanket from under the seat.

"What's going on?" I asked, wrapping it around myself. I folded my legs up so I could warm my toes with the fabric. The two of them shared the other seat, their eyes focused on me.

"I found you in an alley last night, with a man who had a cane and..."

"And a knife," I added, vividly remembering the way it glistened in the light of the moon.

"You remember." Her look was pained and apologetic.

"He stabbed me," I agreed. It wasn't something I was likely to forget any time soon. "More than once, before you came and scared him off. Then you came and carried me to what looked like a large beach house, but I woke up in a very rudimentary hospital room that felt more like a morgue." There were so many things that didn't make sense right now. Perhaps these people were on the wrong side of the law and used a mortician to treat their friends to avoid being reported to the authorities, but I was not their friend.

"He brought you to my house," she agreed. "It was closer than the hospital, and Gabriel here is a doctor." That explained the white lab coat.

"You treated me?" I asked, hoping he would tell me he stitched me back together, as good as new, but even I knew that wasn't possible. I felt the knife pierce my skin last night, but there wasn't even a blemish in its place.

"I wanted to, but we were too late to do much of anything." His jaw was set, like he was trying to be emotionless, but his eyes had lost their intensity and were filled with sorrow.

"You held me in your arms until…until I passed out."

"Until you died," he said delicately.

"You don't wake up from being dead," I argued.

"You don't wake up healed the day after a monster shreds your insides either." The woman, Cassandra, said this with a hatred directed at William, before she turned to me, her eyes wide. "I'm sorry, this is scary and confusing and I'm not helping."

"It's impossible," I argued with her assessment.

"It's a lot to process," Gabriel said.

"It's insane," I told him. "Why aren't the two of you freaking out? By your own account, you watched me die last night, yet I am sitting in front of you now and neither of you looks the least bit disturbed."

"Loretta," Cassandra reached towards me, but I pulled my hands back.

"How do you know my name?" Suspicion filled me with terror. I felt more alone and vulnerable than I ever had before last night.

"When we brought you to the hospital last night, the doctor on duty recognized you. He said you worked for him last year," Gabriel explained.

"But you don't work at the hospital, do you?" I called him on it.

"Not usually, but today I was doing a favor for a friend." He eyed Cassie, but I couldn't quite read the look. There was sadness and regret, but also guilt.

"That still doesn't explain why you're acting like this is normal," I brought the conversation back to my apparent resurrection.

"Because it happened to me," Gabriel said.

I don't know what I was expecting, but it definitely wasn't that.

"How?" I asked.

"I'm not sure," he shrugged apologetically. "But you're not alone."

"Let's go inside. I'll find you a dress and Gabriel can tell you what he knows," Cassie said when the carriage stopped.

"I want to go home." I shook my head and refused to move.

"That's not a good idea."

"You can't keep me here against my will." I felt the fear from last night coming back.

"No, you're free to go wherever you want, but according to the rest of the world, you died last night," Cassandra explained to me. "You're also currently wearing a stranger's coat over what looks like…nothing. At least let me get you some warm clothes."

I COULDN'T ARGUE with her assessment, so I reluctantly followed them through a trail of sand and rocks to get to the house I'd been brought to last night. Now that I was fully conscious, I could see that it was a rather large house with expensive decorations. There was the definitely a house-by-the-sea vibe, but there were also gorgeous and expensive paintings and sculptures.

"Is that an Antonio Canova sculpture?" I asked, still not trusting them, but I had never seen a real one up close. One of my first stops if I ever made it to Paris would be the Louvre. I planned to spend weeks wandering the halls and hours staring at each masterpiece within.

"I believe so. It's Cassie's house," he explained his lack of knowledge.

"You're not her husband?" I was surprised.

"No," he shook his head with a smile like he found the idea hilarious. "I'm a family friend. Her husband travels a lot for business, and he likes to bring back something for her every time he goes. I can talk your ear off about the Vermeer upstairs, but sculptures were never my thing."

"Lucky girl."

"Have you been to Paris?" he asked.

"I know you're trying to distract me, but I have a lot of questions that I need answered."

"Of course. I had a lot of questions as well."

"Who answered them for you?"

"No one," he sighed, taking a seat on what I believe was the couch they put me on last night, but there wasn't even a trace of blood on it. "It was some kind of an illness. I was lucky that it happened during a blizzard, so by the time the snow cleared enough to go get a doctor, I was already awake."

"Then how do you know you died and didn't just get better?"

"Because it happened in 1684."

"You're…"

"Very old," he agreed.

"Are you a vampire? Am I?" I asked. I never thought they were real, but I was doubting everything now. I was absolutely starving, and it felt like my stomach had been digesting itself since I woke up, but I wanted meat and potatoes, not people.

"No. There's no blood sucking, you can walk in the sun…you just don't die."

"Ever?" I asked.

"That part isn't as clear. From what we've gathered, we stay alive until we accomplish something specific. For now, every time I die, I come back to life."

"What are you supposed to do?" I asked, but he could see I was skeptical.

"I'm protecting Cassie," he said with the tiniest smile.

"She looks like she can take care of herself."

"She definitely can," he agreed. "It's not just Cassie. Her ancestor was my best friend, and the love of my life, so before she died, I promised to protect her daughter. Only I said it in a way that implied I would protect all of her descendants."

"That's an interesting promise to make. When my parents died, my sister promised to take care of me, but I'm pretty sure she just meant until I came of age," I shared, but thinking of Georgina made my heart hurt.

"It's a long story," he waved it off.

"What's my purpose?" I asked him.

"I don't know. That's something you have to figure out."

"How?"

"Some people never do."

"Your theory is that I died last night, then came back to life this afternoon so that I can accomplish some magical task I may never figure out?"

"I'm open to hear if you have any better explanations."

"But you're sure I died?"

"Your wounds are gone, aren't they? Not healed, but gone as if they never happened?"

"I just…I need to go home and see my sister," I said instead of answering him, but he knew he was right.

"I'm not going to stop you, but generally, unless no one knows that you died, going home doesn't work."

"They're all I have," I argued.

"You have us now." Cassandra came and gave me a pile of clothes.

I didn't say anything as I followed her to an empty room and put on the dress she gave me. It was beautiful, the kind of thing Georgina usually wore. Before last night, I would have been so excited to wear something so fancy and clearly expensive, but today it just magnified how much I did not belong here.

. . .

"Mrs. Lovell made us some tea and snacks." Cassandra brought me to another room and showed me a spread of treats and tiny sandwiches, as well as a couple of teapots that the older woman from last night was setting up. "I figured you must be starving." Cassandra had a motherly tone to her, but there didn't seem to be any children around. Instead, the hallway had a suit of armor and a rack of swords that looked entirely out of place in the holiday house, and incredibly unsafe, even for adults.

I was going to say I wasn't hungry and try to leave, not needing to know why she had so many weapons on display, but my stomach made a very loud gurgling noise.

"I'll see if we have something more substantial," Mrs. Lovell offered.

"This is fine," I assured her, devouring the scones in a way my mother definitely would not have approved of. I then proceeded to eat more than my fair share of the sandwiches.

"I'm going to leave now, but thank you for saving me last night, and for the dress. I'll return it as soon as I get my own," I said as soon as the plates were empty, giving Cassie back her wool blanket. I half-expected the suit of armor to come to life and block my way. Stranger things had happened lately.

"You don't have to leave," Cassandra told me instead, as if she truly wanted me to stay.

"I do," I argued, resigned. "I'm sorry."

CHAPTER FIVE

Once I was outside, I thought I would feel free, but getting away from Gabriel and Cassandra didn't make me feel any better. I was equally confused, but now I was also alone. I had to get home to Georgina.

Walking gave me more than enough time to think about everything that happened. Leaving Cassie's property required all of my attention so I wouldn't twist my ankle, but my thoughts were able to wander once I got closer to town. I was so focused on what today's developments meant that I hadn't processed what happened last night. The dying and coming back to life were the main events, but before that, I was nearly raped. By William.

"Miss?" I was shaken from my thoughts by a blond man who towered over me. By the tone and volume of his voice, I would assume he'd tried to get my attention more than once.

"Yes?" I asked, pulling the morgue technician's coat closer around myself as if it could protect me from him.

"I'm so sorry to bother you, but I saw you walking by and…I wanted to make sure you were okay."

"What? I'm…I'm fine," I said, trying to get past him. The sun was setting, and I did not want to be out alone at night again.

"You don't look it. I mean, you look fine, in that sense, but something is clearly troubling you." He was flustered, but also worried about me.

"It's really none of your concern." I didn't mean to be rude, because he genuinely looked like he cared, but he was a large man and I was not interested in a repeat of last night. Even if Gabriel thought I would survive it.

"I know. I'm sorry. I've just seen that look before and…I couldn't forgive myself if I let it happen to someone else."

"What look?" I asked, ready to give him a piece of my mind.

"You look lost. Devastated. Like something just happened that made you question everything in your life. You seem alone and terrified about what comes next. I don't know your story or what's going on, but I do know that you shouldn't be alone."

"I'm not alone," I lied, shocked by how well he'd read my expression.

"I know," he assured me, but his look told me he also knew the truth.

"I'm going to leave now," I told him.

"Of course." He was nervous and nodding his head like he was trying to reconcile himself with that concept.

"Goodbye," I said, pushing past him.

"Do you mind if I keep you company?" He turned around and called after me.

"I don't know you," I argued.

"My name is Caleb Fletcher. I was born and raised in Texas. I'm in town for a few days with a friend who wanted to check in on a family member who's going through a tough time. I was in the army for a bit, and my favorite pie is apple," he told me, holding his hands up to show he meant me no harm.

"I don't mean to be rude, and I appreciate what you're trying to do, but right now, you're the biggest threat for me in these streets, and you might know that you're not going to hurt me, but I've recently been shown that my instincts about people are terribly wrong, so I would feel safer if I was walking the streets alone, rather than with another man."

Regret passed his face, like he suddenly understood my look, and wished he could have done something to prevent it.

"In that case do you mind if I stay back, far enough that you don't need to worry about me, but close enough that no one else will bother you?"

I considered it, but something about him made me trust him. His eyes were like Gabriel's, so dark I could swear they were black, but there was an intense kindness to them that caught me off guard.

"Okay," I reluctantly agreed. "But anything closer than fifty feet and I'm running away screaming like you couldn't imagine."

"Understood," he assured me.

AT FIRST IT FELT ODD. That feeling you get when you're walking alone, like someone is following you, was ominously present, but I knew where it was coming from, so it wasn't as terrifying. I was far from comfortable, but I felt like nothing other than Caleb was going to get to me tonight, and for some reason, that was reassuring.

WE MADE it to the front gate, at which point I turned back and found Caleb probably exactly fifty feet away from me, walking like he had all the time in the world and wasn't inconvenienced in the least by following me home like a guard dog who couldn't be trusted close to children.

"This is me," I told him.

"Thank you for letting me walk you home."

"You take care now." I told him, shutting the gate behind me. I walked up the familiar path to the house, but I had feelings of dread and terror that weren't familiar at all.

I could feel Caleb's eyes on me, watching to make sure I made it inside, but I stopped once I reached the front windows.

Georgina was standing there, holding her muddy green shawl in her hands, crying. I was relieved to see Bruno had made his way back. He was sitting at her feet, drawn to her pain. Billy and Catherine were playing somewhere I couldn't see, but I could hear their squeals of joy. Every time their laughter got louder, Georgina looked like the hole in her heart grew a little bigger. She let out a long sob of despair, hunched over and clutching the shawl to her chest, then William came into the frame of the window and took her in his arms. I couldn't hear what he was saying to her, but he rubbed her back, held her close, and consoled her over my death. Which he caused.

I HAD COME to see my sister and that was still what I wanted, more than anything, but the scene in front of me implied someone had told her what happened last night. Obviously not all of the details, because William was still walking free. No matter how relieved and happy she would be to see me if I knocked on the door, she would have a million questions that I couldn't answer. And William would never let me get close to her. He killed me once to keep his secret, so I doubted he would hesitate to do it a second time.

I took a deep breath and wiped the tears that were falling down my face, but more replaced them almost immediately. I turned and walked back to the road, not sure where I was going to go, but knowing home was no longer an option. My tears blurred my vision to the point that I didn't even see Caleb's six-foot frame until I nearly walked into him.

"Woah there," he said, gently preventing the collision.

"Why are you still here?" I asked through the tears.

"I was taught to wait until the person got inside before accepting that they would be safe, and you never went inside," he explained.

"It's the wrong house," I said.

"I've been there," he agreed.

"Inside that house?" I asked, pretty sure I would have remembered him.

"Not exactly," he said, looking at me in a way that implied he meant where I was emotionally. "I went off to war a mama's boy who playfully teased his sisters and had a head full of hopes and dreams. When I finally made it home, I...the war changed me, in all the usual ways, but also in ways I had never expected. I found myself staring into my living room window, watching them, when it hit me that I never really made it home."

"What did you do?" I asked. You couldn't exactly compare how you feel after killing people and seeing death to being dead and not able to talk to your family without shocking them to death, but there might be some cross over.

"I stayed there a really long time, watching them. Half-hoping someone would notice me, but knowing it would be better if they didn't. Eventually, I just grabbed my bag and left."

"You never went inside?"

"I couldn't." His face got dark for a moment, and I had an overwhelming urge to move closer and put my hand on his arm. "But I still think about it. All the time."

"If you could go back now, would you go in?" I asked.

"I think it's too late for me, but you still have time."

"I can't," I argued.

"I wasn't trying to push you. I just know from experience that whatever it is you think you did that was so horrible, chances are they would rather have you back than whatever it is you're considering."

"It's never too late for family," I told him, retracing my steps to the gate.

"You're not going back?" Caleb asked me.

"There's something I have to do first."

CHAPTER SIX

I let Caleb find me a carriage and gave the driver turn-by-turn directions when I couldn't provide an address. I hadn't realized how far I walked, but it was pitch black outside, so I had to rely on memory rather than landmarks, which was not my strong suit.

Eventually, I made it to the large and imposing house. It wasn't until the carriage drove away that I realized Cassie might already be in bed, and I might not be welcome. The lights were on, however, so I decided to chance it.

I walked up to the imposing front doors and knocked to announce my presence. It took forever before I heard footsteps.

"Loretta," Cassandra said with a relieved smile when she opened the door. "We were worried about you." The words weren't even out of her mouth when she took me in for a hug. I was surprised at first, but it was the first hug I'd received since my death. I hadn't realized how much I'd missed them. It had barely been twenty-four hours, but a lot had happened.

· · ·

WHEN THE HUG ENDED, she brought me to the fireplace so I could warm up, keeping a hand on my shoulder as we sat on the dreadful couch I died on.

"You were right." I tried to bury down the emotions. "I couldn't go home."

"If I had known you were like Gabriel, I would have kept you here last night instead of bringing you to the hospital. It could have given you a few more years," she apologized.

"That's not why," I assured her. "I mean, the world believing I'm dead doesn't help, but I couldn't go home even if Gabriel had somehow managed to nurse me back to health." I wrapped my arms tighter around myself, fighting off a chill that had nothing to do with how cold it was outside.

"The man who did this to you?" Cassie asked.

I nodded, wondering how I could explain what happened when I couldn't process it myself. "If I go home, he will kill me. If I tell my sister what happened, he will kill me. For now, anything other than staying away puts the people I love in danger. I need to find a way to let the world know what he did so he can be locked up or...I don't know, but I can't go home while he's there."

She was nodding along in support, until my last sentence, when her eyes widened. "He's at your home?" she asked.

"He's my brother-in-law," I admitted, before telling her exactly what happened last night. "I'm sorry I didn't tell you, it just didn't make sense, I couldn't believe that he..." I struggled to find the words, but all I got was tears, that burned my eyes and made it so I couldn't see anything clearly.

"You'll be safe here," Cassie assured me.

"But my sister's not," I argued. "You saw him last night. I know it puts a target on your back, but if you could just come with me to the constabulary..."

"They'll know you were dead," she said gently.

"I don't need to go in," I tried.

"Of course, I'll go," she assured me after a heavy sigh. "My husband just got in from his business trip a few hours ago. We can leave as soon as he wakes up."

"It has to be now," I argued. I couldn't stand the idea of William being out there, hurting other women. We needed to go now, while he was at home comforting my sister. I wanted him rotting in a cell.

"Well, we mustn't keep a lady waiting." A man poked his head over the railing before coming down the stairs to join us. "Alan Roosevelt," he introduced himself to me.

"Loretta Crane," I reciprocated, taking his outstretched hand.

"Let's put away a monster, shall we?"

CHAPTER SEVEN

Their driver, Mr. Lovell, was very convincing when he assured us it was no trouble to bring us to the constabulary in the middle of the night.

On the ride, I answered all of their questions about my relationship with William. How I was practically a child when I moved in with him and my sister, how I never thought of him as anything other than a brother. I was in tears when I recounted how he tried to rape me, but stopped when I threatened to tell my sister, until he realized she was going to find out unless he killed me.

I also determined that Alan was not the type to prevent his wife from anything she decided to do, not that I think he could have, but he was intrigued by it.

"Did you get a good look at him?" Alan asked Cassie as we walked down the street to the constabulary.

"It was dark, so I didn't see much, but now that I know his name, it shouldn't be too hard to—"

"You need to be confident, without a doubt, that it's him, or he'll be able to fight it," I warned. I wasn't sure her word would be enough when put against his.

Alan, who was ahead of us, looked back and said something to me, but I froze and didn't hear a word of it. At first because I saw a sketch of my face on the wall promising a reward for anyone who had information on my killer. Then I saw William, in uniform, smoking a cigarette by the door.

"Is everything okay?" Alan asked, coming closer to me.

"We need to leave," I said, trying to swallow, to calm myself down, but my mouth was dry, and it felt like the air had left my body. Even from a distance, I could see cuts from last night on his face. They were thin and deep, as if Georgina had finally caved and let Billy get a cat.

As William looked out into the street, I stepped back and bumped into Alan. Instead of apologizing, I pressed my body against the stone wall, praying he hadn't seen me.

I could tell Alan's first instinct was to coax me to keep moving, but now he looked concerned. I turned to Cassie, hoping the fear and pleading in my eyes would be enough so we could leave, but I could see she'd recognized him as well.

"Let's go home," she decided, but I saw William coming towards us and pulled them into a neighboring doorway instead.

"Coming out tonight, Will?" I recognized the voice of Felix, William's best friend.

"Not tonight," William turned him down.

"Oh, come on then, a couple of hours won't hurt."

"I just want to go home to my wife, and my kids, and be there with them."

I could feel the tears, mostly from anger, burning my eyes, but I wiped them before they could fall. Hopefully before Cassie or Alan saw them.

"WHAT JUST HAPPENED?" Alan asked when I released them.

"He was there," Cassie explained, trying not to be reproachful of me, but I hadn't given them all the facts.

"The constables already arrested him?" Alan turned back as if he'd be able to see William through the walls.

"No." Cassie was talking to her husband, but she kept her eyes on me. "He *was* the constable."

"He was at home when I left, so I thought it was our opportunity to come when he wasn't here, but seeing him, and my face in there...I think it will take a lot more than your word for them to believe you."

"We still need to tell someone." Alan was upset, and his concern warmed my heart.

Cassie brought her hand to his cheek and gave him a small smile. "Darling, we live in a world where a woman's opinion is worth maybe half that of a man's. It was already going to be difficult, but if it comes down to my word against a constable, when accusing him of stabbing his sister-in-law to death, no one is going to take my side."

"I would. Your side is the truth," he said like it was a simple matter of facts.

"And that's one of the many reasons why I love you, but the rest of the world will not see it that way."

"You're going to give up?" I would have thought Alan would be relieved, but he was shocked.

"We can't," I argued.

"I am going to find a way to make sure that man never hurts another woman, but I am not going to do it in that station." I got the feeling she would burn the building down if she thought it would help, but she was smart enough to know it wouldn't.

"You're not going to..." I asked, letting the question trail off. I knew William was a monster who needed to pay for his crime, but I wanted him locked up where he couldn't hurt anyone else. I didn't want Cassie to kill him.

"No, I'm sure there's another way. Hopefully one that is less morally suspect, and will show others that it is not a good idea to prey against the weak and vulnerable," she assured me.

"I know you don't like to hear this, but you are one of them," Alan reminded his wife.

"Only in name," she said in a way that left no room for discussion.

CHAPTER EIGHT

JANUARY 6TH, 1843

When I woke up the following morning, Mrs. Lovell had an assortment of breakfast foods waiting on the table, including pancakes, porridge, fresh fruit and toasts with various jams.

I poured myself a cup of tea, but didn't even add milk or sugar, not sure my stomach could handle anything right now. The cute butterflies people talk about when they're excited had turned into violent moths tinged with fear and apprehension.

"Good morning, Loretta," Gabriel said with a forced smile as he walked in and sat down across from me, followed by Cassie and Alan. I could tell by the look on her face that she'd told Gabriel everything I hadn't, about William being a constable as well as my brother-in-law. Which meant we needed a new plan.

"Good morning." I gave my best attempt at happy, normal behavior.

"Gabriel is going home now Alan's back, but I'm working on a plan. I sent word to some friends, to see if William's done this before, and which constables might be willing to help us share the truth." I could tell Cassie was being optimistic for my benefit, but there were dark circles under her eyes I hadn't noticed before.

"I told you I could stay," Gabriel reminded her, looking concerned.

"Embry's in town, so it works out perfectly," she shared, making Gabriel look both relieved and angry at the same time. "Loretta and I can figure this out while you help Delia." She had a lot more confidence than I did.

"Who's Delia?" I asked, remembering the name from the night they found me.

"She's another Gifted who often patrols with me," Cassie shared. "Delia needs help finding someone, and no one covers more ground faster than Gabriel. He forgets that I take care of myself just fine when he isn't here."

"No, I remember how much you enjoy causing me grief. I'm not as young as I look," Gabriel warned affectionately.

"I wonder who gave her the idea that she could make a difference by saving people in need," Alan said without looking up from the pancakes he was covering in syrup.

"That's different," Gabriel argued.

"How? Delia has told me countless stories about the two of you travelling the world looking for people to help."

"But Delia and I have already died. We have the luxury of giving our lives to the cause, then still having a life."

It sounded like this was an argument they had often, although my money was on Gabriel being the one who always gave in. It was interesting because while Alan saw Cassie as his partner and encouraged her, understanding it was who she was, Gabriel saw her as someone he needed to protect. Which didn't really seem to be the case.

"I'll come back once we find her," Gabriel said with a sigh, rising from the table without eating more than a few spoons full of porridge.

"Agree to disagree?" Cassie asked him without getting up from the table.

"As always. But do try to be safe," he asked of her, kissing the top of her head.

"Of course," she said innocently, but I knew she was planning something.

CHAPTER NINE

When I came down after getting dressed, there was a man in the entrance, with a faint Italian accent. He embraced Cassandra like a beloved niece, even though they looked the same age.

"This is Embry," Cassie introduced me. "And this is my dear friend, Loretta."

"My friends call me Lorie," I told her. After saving my life, watching me die and housing me, it seemed only fair.

"He's like you and Gabriel," she gave me a pointed look before going inside.

"You're Gifted?" Embry asked without losing his smile.

"I don't think I would call it that," I argued.

"It's what they call us, because we have Gifts," he explained.

"I didn't get anything. In fact, I woke up in a morgue with nothing."

"That's rough," he cocked his head to the side and sighed. "I meant Gifts like Gabriel's speed," he said it like I should know what he was talking about.

"Is that how he got to us so fast?" I asked, turning to Cassie. She was giving us space, but she was clearly still listening.

"I'm on my own all the time when he's not here, but that was the only way he would let us separate. No matter where he was, it would take less than a minute for him to get to me once he saw the flare," she agreed.

"What can you do?" I asked Embry.

"He manipulates feelings," Alan said, bringing Embry a glass of scotch. "Would you like one?" he offered me.

"No thank you," I assured him before rounding on Embry. "You play with peoples' feelings?"

"He said it like that to get you worried. I can influence how the people around me feel, but I mostly just bring comfort and happiness to people who are suffering," he said like it was nothing, but he gave Cassandra a look that she dismissed with a smile.

"But you could do incredible damage," I realized. "You could put someone into a blind rage, or make them paranoid and lose trust in the people around them...you could make someone so desperate that they—"

"I could," he cut me off, "but I don't. I might convince people to turn a blind eye, or believe me when I'm clearly lying, but I don't use my Gift to kill. Unless I can't help it."

"In that case, I'm not like them," I told Cassie.

"I haven't met anyone who wakes up after being dead, other than Gifteds," she argued.

"I have no athletic abilities and if I had any power over the people around me, William would have left my sister and dropped dead," I said the words and was pretty sure I meant them, but I still couldn't reconcile the monster from the other night with the man who helped my sister raise me, and doted on his children.

"You'll figure it out soon enough," Embry assured me. "Some Gifts are obvious, but others take some time. We all have them though."

"How many of you are there?"

"It's hard to tell. Thousands at least, but probably more."

"And what's the point? So star-crossed lovers can keep their promises?"

36

"Some people have more exciting stories. My friend died for the first time of smallpox when he was barely a man, then spent decades trying everything to discover his purpose. He helped win the war of independence and write the U.S. Constitution, dying at least a dozen times from drowning, diseases and battle wounds, before he finally achieved it by founding the nation."

"Are you talking about our first president, George Washington?" I asked, but surely he didn't really mean that one of the Founding Fathers was Gifted.

"Yes, but we just called him George."

I digested this information for a moment, trying to decide if I believed him, then wondered what I was meant to do. "I assume my job is to bring down William so he can't hurt anyone else?"

"It could be," Embry agreed after a look to Cassandra.

"What happens when you do whatever it is you're supposed to do?" I asked.

"I'm not sure. Some say you get to live out the rest of your life as you were meant to, one woman told me a white tunnel appeared, calling to her...others have just never woken up."

"Never woken up?" I asked.

"It's not that Gifted can't die; we just tend to wake up when we do. Sometimes our Gifts change when that happens, possibly as a punishment or a reward based on our behavior, but I don't think there's a reason to it."

"But sometimes..." I pressed.

"Sometimes we don't wake up, even if we haven't finished what we were supposed to do. I mean, maybe they accomplished it without figuring out what it was, but from their perspective, they just don't wake up."

CHAPTER TEN

After lunch, Cassandra revealed her plan; talk to my sister while William was at work.

"She won't listen to you," I argued. "I was there when he…I saw it with my own eyes and I'm still not sure I believe it sometimes. She definitely won't take the word of a stranger over her own husband."

"I'll go with her," Embry said delicately.

"No," I refused. "You can't just play mind games on her. We're trying to protect her, not manipulate her."

"I won't do anything other than make her clear-headed and open minded."

"I'll make sure of it," Cassie added.

"I should come with you. If you're going to play games with her mind, you might as well just make her not freak out when she sees me."

"I would have to use it on your niece and nephew as well, and they would be in danger if things don't go as planned, because they would all be witnesses to the fact that you're sort of still alive."

"Then what am I supposed to do while you try to turn my sister against her husband?" I knew it had to be done, but I didn't think the two of them going without me was the solution.

"You can take Mr. Lovell and wait outside the constabulary. If you see William leave and head home, you come warn us."

"I don't like this plan," I argued.

"Our best bet at getting him away from your sister is to make sure she knows what kind of man he is. Even if we get him arrested or sent to jail, it won't matter if she stands by him and believes his innocence," Cassie reminded me.

I knew she was right, so I reluctantly nodded.

WE ALL WENT OUTSIDE TOGETHER, but Embry and Cassandra took one of her carriages to my house, while Mr. Lovell used the other to bring me back to the constabulary. Instead of waiting outside in the cold, he waited inside with me.

"How long have you been working for Cassandra?" I asked him after a few minutes in silence. He and his wife were either very loyal, or paid incredibly well, given Cassie's extracurricular activities. Not to mention how well Mrs. Lovell took it when I died on the sofa one night and was a dinner guest the next.

"Since she was a little girl. My wife was hired when Miss Cassie's mother died, and I was brought on not long after," he shared. There was pride and love in his voice when he mentioned Cassie.

"Were you surprised when you found out about…everything?" I couldn't find a succinct way to reference all that was going on in Cassie's world.

"It came on gradually," he assured me.

"I can't imagine ever being that brave and daring," I shared, knowing that if our roles had been reversed that night, I would have run for help, but definitely not towards the danger.

"Believe it or not, the crime-fighting was harder to accept than people reincarnating."

"Really?" I smiled, but I couldn't believe that the impossible would be more surprising than a strong and independent woman.

"Not like that," he defended himself. "When I met her, Miss Cassie was a shy, soft-spoken lass who I expected to marry some high-ranking soldier or aristocrat and spend the rest of her life raising bairns and entertaining. Not that there's anything wrong with that. More than once she had me come investigate a scary noise, kill a bug for her, or adjust the carriage a half-dozen times so the ground would be dry and she wouldn't get her shoes dirty."

"That's…that doesn't sound like her."

"My daughter, Genevieve, she had an awful stutter when she was little, so she usually chose to stay silent, and didn't really have many friends."

"Until Cassie?" I guessed.

"She immediately took Gen under her wing, and her protection. Her voice got stronger when she used it in the defense of others, and things she couldn't do for herself, she could do effortlessly for someone else. She became a guardian angel, not only to Gen, but to every helpless soul she encountered."

"There's a difference between speaking up for someone being teased and getting into a fight with a drunk man twice your size," I argued.

"Which is why many of us spend a lot of sleepless nights praying for Miss Cassie." He gave me a knowing smile.

"She's lucky to have you."

"Family comes in all shapes and sizes, but we all play our parts," he shrugged it off.

"Is your daughter…" I started, hoping it wasn't too forward.

"She got married on Christmas Eve, so she's spending a few weeks with the in-laws. Gabriel stayed after the wedding, but usually Gen is the one who follows Miss Cassie into the night on dangerous adventures." I could tell he didn't like it, but I also think he was proud.

I was going to ask him more about Cassie's wild lifestyle, but I saw William walk out of the constabulary.

"Is that him?" Mr. Lovell asked.

I nodded. "He doesn't seem to be going home though," I pointed out when William headed in the opposite direction.

"Miss Cassie said I shouldn't let you out of the carriage," Mr. Lovell argued when I tried to go outside.

"And would Miss Cassie listen to that?" I asked, trying to channel Cassie's confidence.

Before he could answer, I opened the door and disappeared into the crowd, determined to find my courage.

CHAPTER ELEVEN

I followed William through the busy streets. Luckily, it was cold enough, with a biting wind, that no one thought twice about me using a shawl to cover my face. When I saw him walk into the pub, I considered going back to the carriage now I knew where he was, but I couldn't risk him leaving and sneaking past us.

My decision to guard the door worked much better in theory, however. The shawl was no longer simply a ruse to hide my face, it was the only thing preventing my ears from falling off, and I wasn't sure how much longer I could trust it.

After a few minutes, I found myself staring longingly through the window, where I could see a fireplace roaring and warm dishes like chicken pot pie being served.

I was scanning the area for a shop I could go into where they didn't know me, and no one would mind me seeking refuge from the cold, but most establishments wouldn't stand for that.

"Permission to approach?" I recognized Caleb's voice and couldn't help but smile.

"You may," I assured him, turning around. I was yet again surprised by the depth of his dark eyes.

"Forgive me, I didn't get your name." He was smiling, and looked way too happy to see me for the heaviness of our last conversation.

"Loretta Crane," I shared, only because I knew he was from out of town. Even then, I would have to come up with a new name next time someone asked.

"Pleased to meet you, Etta" he did a slight bow. I was going to correct him, assuming he misunderstood, but his smile told me I'd just been given a new nickname. And I liked it. "Are you waiting for someone?" he looked around at the mostly empty streets. Everyone else who was out had a clear purpose. None of them were just standing outside a shop, debating whether or not they should go in.

"No, of course not." It was only partly a lie. I wasn't waiting for William so much as waiting to see where he went.

"In that case, could I offer you a warm beverage? Or even a meal, if that isn't too forward. I was just about to get something at the hotel." He nodded off to the distance, where his hotel must be.

I considered it, and decided this was another way for me to find my courage. "What about this place?" I motioned to the ale house. "It smells wonderful," I managed to say it convincingly, even if the smell of food was currently masked by the smell of stale alcohol, and musk.

"I would be delighted," he said, only slightly judging me for it.

I WORE my shawl around my head until we were seated in a corner, where I had a perfect view of the back of William's head, but he would have to turn around and crane his neck to see me.

"Are you warm enough?" Caleb asked after removing his overcoat, clearly about to offer it to me.

"The fire is lovely." I had that same paralyzing fear from last night at being so close to William, knowing he could discover me at any moment, but Caleb's easy smile and attitude were slowly convincing my breathing to slow down to a normal rhythm.

"Have you been here before then?" he asked, looking around.

"No, never," I said a little too quickly. Other than the fireplace, which was inviting, I never would have approached this establishment if it weren't for my current mission. "How is your trip going? Did your friend help their friend?"

"I hope so. He's been off all day, so I've taken in the sights."

"There aren't very many," I said, trying to think of what I would show someone who'd never been here before. "Although sunrises and sunsets are magical by the water."

"Some sights make up for others," he said, looking at me in a way that definitely made me blush. I could feel the heat rising in my cheeks, and hoped he associated it with the heat from the fireplace.

I ALMOST GOT LOST in the conversation with Caleb, but always found my way back to William's table, to make sure he was still there. He was drinking with a couple of men I didn't recognize, but he seemed rather friendly with them.

"Do you know them?" Caleb asked me.

"Not really." It didn't even feel like a lie.

"I can be a very good listener," he volunteered himself.

"He's married to a friend of mine," I decided to stay as close to the truth as I could.

"And he shouldn't be in here?" he guessed.

"He shouldn't be anywhere," I said under my breath, but Caleb was looking at me expectantly. "Have you ever known something so terrible that it would destroy someone? Like shatter their heart into a million pieces and make them question everything they've ever known?"

"Is he the man who made the streets feel dangerous to you?" he found a delicate way of asking a terrible question. I forgot what I had told him, and instantly regretted it when I saw his hands close into fists.

"It has nothing to do with me," I lied. "Other than the fact that I saw him with another woman."

"And you want to go over there and confront him?" he asked, thinking he figured out why I'd been waiting outside on my own.

"I want to protect her," I simplified it, only it really wasn't simple.

"You haven't told her," he understood.

"I don't have any proof. Just my word against his."

"Are you more afraid of her getting hurt, or of having her believe him instead of you?"

"You don't know what you're talking about." I don't think he meant anything by it, other than making conversation, but I felt attacked. Of course, I wanted to protect Georgina, more than anything. And I was reluctant to break her heart with the earth-shattering news Cassie and Embry were currently delivering. Part of me knew she would believe it more from someone like me than from a stranger, but I also knew that it would break my heart all over again, and so much worse, if I told her what he did to me, but she still took his side.

"I'm sorry," Caleb apologized, just as William headed for the door.

"I have to go," I told him before hurrying after William, to the carriage.

"WE NEED TO WARN THEM; he's going home," I told Mr. Lovell as soon as I was close enough that he would hear me.

"They just rode through. I said you were gone into the boutique to use the restroom. Embry knew I was lying, of course, but he didn't say anything."

I breathed a sigh of relief. "Thank you," I told him.

"Of course," he assured me. "Glad ye're okay."

"WHAT HAPPENED WITH MY SISTER?" I asked Cassandra once I got to her house.

"She answered our questions, but even when Embry tried to make her suspicious, she never once doubted her husband."

She explained how they asked where he was, how he'd been

45

acting lately, all kinds of leading questions, but Georgie shot them down every time they hinted at anything, finding the suggestion ridiculous.

"Is she okay? How are the kids?" It was killing me that I couldn't be with them right now.

"They're…" she looked at me with pity. "They're exactly what you would expect of someone who just lost one of their favorite people in the world. Smiles are hard to come by, toys are less exciting…but they've got each other and they're healing."

"Thank you," I told her.

"There's nothing to be thankful for," she assured me.

"You told the truth," I argued. "Most people wouldn't have."

"A lie to make someone feel better is still a lie. It just delays the truth," she shrugged.

CHAPTER TWELVE

JANUARY 7TH, 1843

The next morning, I set out before the others woke up, to deliver a letter to an old friend of Georgina's. I didn't know how much weight my word carried, when Georgina was aware I died days ago, but other than William and I, Simon Davenport was the only family we had. He grew up in the house next to ours, until he went away for school. He was at Georgina's wedding, and my parents' funeral, but I hadn't seen him more than a handful of times since he was elected to the senate. It was a long shot, but I had to hope that even an anonymous letter accusing the man married to his oldest friend of heinous crimes would warrant some kind of investigation. He was probably the only living person that my sister would believe, but even then, if Embry's Gift hadn't worked, I wasn't getting my hopes up.

I left the letter at Simon's office, and was going to walk back to Cassie's, when I saw Caleb purchasing a newspaper across the street.

"Mr. Fletcher," I called, walking over.

"Miss Crane." I was relieved when he smiled at the sight of me.

"I wanted to apologize for yesterday. My feelings weren't directed at you –"

"I hope some of them were," he teased, making me blush again.

"Not the angry, defensive ones."

"Apology accepted," he assured me. "Where were you headed?"

"Home, actually."

"Can I accompany you?" he offered. "Or possible take you on a detour to get some food?"

It took me less than a second to consider it. "I would very much like that." I took a deep breath, but my nerves were from excitement, not fear.

WE WALKED to the outskirts of town before finding a spot to eat. I could have spent hours talking to him like that, but I needed to get us away from anyone who could recognize me. I did not need a witch hunt after me, on top of everything else.

AFTER THE MEAL, he again offered to walk me home, and I agreed, wanting nothing more than to spend more time with him. I headed towards Cassie's, while he went the other way, towards my actual home. "I'm staying with a friend until…"

"Until you can go home," he finished for me with a comforting smile. My breath caught in my chest when he took my hand in his, but then my entire body relaxed.

THE WALK from Cassie's had taken me less than an hour this morning, but we had travelled in the opposite direction to eat, and we took our sweet time, stopping into shops that I could enter while completely bundled up, never staying long enough to need to remove the shawl that covered most of my face. The sun was setting by the time we got back to Simon's office.

"I appreciate you doing this," I told Caleb as we slowly made our way across town. Now that I knew him better, there really was no one else I would rather walk down a dark alley with. Except maybe Cassandra, but she didn't have the benefit of looking like an imposing lumberjack.

"It's truly my pleasure. And I would never forgive myself if anything happened to you," he said, looking down so he could stare into my eyes, making my heart beat faster.

"Where were you three nights ago?" I asked, shaking my head, mostly to break some of the electricity that had been building between us all day.

"On my way to you," he said it teasingly, but his eyes told me he meant it.

He leaned in, ever so slowly, and I froze. The part of my brain that understood what was going on with the Gifted and me being dead told me I should stay away, that this was a bad idea, but the rest of it, the part that was still Loretta and couldn't believe she finally met the man of her dreams, that part closed her eyes and waited for the fireworks.

Instead of the kiss I'd been dreaming about, I heard the terrified scream of a woman, coming from one of the other alleys. Caleb heard it too and pulled away from me.

"We need to help her," I told him.

"I'll go to her. You get help. There's a constabulary nearby," he told me before running off in the direction her screams were coming from. The situation was eerily familiar, giving me the overwhelming urge to vomit on the side of the street, but I refrained myself.

I appreciated Caleb's concern, but I wasn't the weak and innocent woman I had been a few nights before. I was apparently Gifted, and while I wasn't sure how much I believed Gabriel's theory, I would feel a lot less guilty if I ran to her help with Caleb than if I stood there and did nothing. Because I was pretty sure William was on duty tonight, and the last thing I wanted to do was bring him to a woman who was scared and alone in a dark alley at night. I knew from experience that it wouldn't end well.

I followed the screams to a woman who was surrounded, not just by one worthless creep, but a whole gang of burly men. Caleb was distracting them for the moment, but there were six of them, and only one of him. He was by far the tallest, and strongest, but it looked like he was holding himself back; hitting them hard enough to momentarily incapacitate them, but not enough to kill or permanently injure them.

I took advantage of their fight to go over and make sure the woman was okay. She looked to be about sixteen or seventeen years old, with tousled blond hair. Her face had a smear of blood on it, probably from wiping her split lip, and her dress was ripped at the seams down the middle, exposing her corset.

"Are you okay?" I asked, taking off my shawl and wrapping it around her.

She nodded, shivering, but other than not being dead, she was definitely not okay.

I got her to her feet and followed her gaze to the fight, which was no longer in Caleb's favor. His refusal to put any of the men out of commission meant that they kept coming back and ganging up on him. I assumed that was what made him tired and slowed him down, until I saw a glint of moonlight on a blade and realized he'd been stabbed.

The woman saw this too, so instead of sticking around for them to bring their attention back to her, she ran into the safety of the streets, limping and only wearing one shoe. I wanted to call after her and offer her some kind of help, but I couldn't leave Caleb behind.

I took an assessment of the six men and saw I knew four of them. William was still in uniform, brandishing his knife like he knew how to use it and wanted the world to see. Felix came behind Caleb and grabbed his arms so he couldn't fight back anymore. Murphy and Colt both worked in the shipyard. I didn't know them in relation to William, other than him frequently warning Georgina and I to stay away from them, especially if the children were with us.

Murphy, Colt, and the two men I didn't know joined William in attacking Caleb with knives, sticks, and their fists.

"Stop!" I screamed, knowing I was helpless against the six of them, but no one even bothered to turn around, probably assuming my screams were from the woman they'd been violating. Once Caleb's stomach was pierced by three blades at once, they took off.

I rushed to Caleb's side and saw the blood pouring out of his stomach, onto the street beneath him. I closed my eyes hard, trying to block out the memory of my own blood on a similar street, but the memory was waiting for me there as well.

"I'm going to put pressure on your wounds and stop the bleeding, but you need a doctor," I told him, trying to apply pressure to the many holes in his stomach, but failing miserably.

"It's okay," he said, sounding so weak that it scared me even more than all of the blood. And there was a lot.

"No, it's not. You're going to be fine. I just need to get you a doctor and he'll give you stitches, and you'll be as good as new." I was rambling, but I could see the blood was pouring out, soaking through every piece of fabric I used to slow it.

"It's okay, I'm…"

Whatever he was, I wasn't going to find out, because he lost consciousness. His pulse was weak, and I knew that even if I miraculously managed to get him to a hospital, there was little they could do to save him.

CHAPTER THIRTEEN

"You're going to be fine, Caleb, okay?" I said, even though all evidence pointed to the contrary. "You have to be because I have waited a long time to find a guy who is nice and kind and makes me smile, and you just can't die right now, okay?" I kept talking to him, even if he probably couldn't hear me, and the reassurances were most likely lies.

But then something happened.

At first all I felt was heat on my hands, which I wrongfully assumed was from the blood. As the heat grew stronger, I felt a pinch in my stomach, that intensified, until it felt just like when I was stabbed. It happened five more times, all across my abdomen; a searing pain like being sliced into, until I could no longer breathe and felt as weak as Caleb looked.

I tried to keep talking, both to reassure him and so he would know he wasn't alone, but I felt like all of my blood and energy, all of my life was pouring out of me. Right when I felt like I was going to pass out and couldn't take it anymore, the pain stopped, leaving me with an odd feeling in my stomach, and an intense heat in my hands. The world started spinning, so I focused on Caleb, lying in a pool of his own blood, his shirt ripped in multiple places, and I felt like my heart was being ripped out of my chest. I held him close, with his head in my lap, promising him he would be okay, even though I knew it was not at all a promise I could make.

AFTER A FEW MINUTES, I was sure I saw Mr. Lovell rushing towards me, but I must have imagined it. I closed my eyes to try and stop the spinning, but before I got the chance to open them, I went from feeling faint to feeling nothing at all.

CHAPTER FOURTEEN

JANUARY 8TH, 1843

I woke up on Cassandra's dreaded couch, with the sounds of people hurrying around to fetch things. I couldn't see Caleb, but I heard Mrs. Lovell in another room, going on about all the blood and where it came from.

"Where's Caleb? Is he okay?" I asked, standing up way too quickly when I saw Cassie walk by. The sun wasn't up yet, but I could tell it was early morning.

"Easy there," she said, trying to get me to sit back down. "The man they found you with?" she asked me.

"He needs your help. Is Gabriel back?"

"He's still with Delia. When you weren't back for dinner, Alan and Mr. Lovell went looking. They found you in the street, covered in blood," she explained how I got back here. I detected a note of fear in her voice. "Alan and Mrs. Lovell are taking care of your friend."

"Is Alan a doctor?" I asked, confused. All I knew of his job was that it required him to travel, but I wouldn't have thought he was in the medical field.

"No, but your friend doesn't need a doctor. Who is he?" she asked me.

"Caleb Fletcher," I shared. "I met him on the street the other day when I left your house a total mess, and he wouldn't let me walk home alone, even if I didn't trust him. I ran into him yesterday, and then again this morning. The day got away from us, and he was walking me home, but then we heard a woman scream and Caleb tried to fend them off, but there were six of them and they had knives and they killed him." I was sobbing by the end of it, mourning his loss and knowing that it was all my fault. "You have to save him," I cried.

"Of course," she assured me.

"Thank you," I breathed a sigh of relief, then got up and headed for the door.

"Where are you going?" she asked, standing as well.

"I can't stay here, I just got a man killed," I pointed out.

"You're not the bad guy in this," Cassie argued.

"No, but I'm not the good guy either."

"What about when he wakes up and asks for you?" she tried.

"He's better off without me."

I heard her call after me, but I kept walking.

CHAPTER FIFTEEN

I walked towards town, with absolutely no idea where I was going to go. Simon would be an option if by some miracle he hadn't heard about my death, but other than that, I couldn't think of a single place I would be welcome. I'd even lost whatever I was building with Caleb.

My hands were still shaking from the adrenaline and the nerves, so I tried to clasp them into calmness, but they were wet and sticky. I looked down and saw they were covered in blood, so I stepped to the side of the road, where there was a tiny stream.

The water was ice cold, but I held my hands under it well past the point at which they went numb, trying to scrub off all the blood. My fingers were stained an unnatural shade of red it took me too long to realize was just the color of skin that was irritated and nearly frostbitten. At least the sun was starting to peek through the frozen branches that surrounded the path

I went back to walking, with no clue where I was going, but it wasn't long before I heard footsteps. Heavy and purposeful. I would have guessed they were Caleb's if I was going from memory, but he was on Cassie's sofa, weak and pale, determinedly fighting to recover from his stab wounds, that he got because of me. Unless the fever dream was real and he was miraculously healed, but I wasn't sure I believed in miracles anymore.

I picked up the pace, not interested in talking to Alan or Mr. Lovell right now, but the footsteps matched my pace as I heard, "Etta," and froze.

I turned around and saw Caleb running after me like nothing had ever happened to him, only there were holes and blood on his shirt. "What...how... I don't understand," I said, looking around as if the answer was somewhere on the buildings behind me.

"I'm sorry I didn't tell you earlier, but I didn't want to scare you off. I died in 1836, I'm Gifted," he explained, both hands in the air, palms facing me to show he had no weapons, but his arms were enough to incapacitate me without issue.

"You're a friend of Cassandra's?" I asked.

"Never met her before in my life," he shook his head. "But I think you're Gifted too," he told me.

"Why?" I asked, scanning his face, but I was pretty sure neither Alan or Cassandra told him about my death and resurrection.

"I've never met someone with Gifts in their first life, but you healed me," he said, lifting his shirt to reveal his flawless skin and taut abs.

"If you're Gifted, that's just what happens when you wake up," I argued, revealing myself.

"I am down to a few hours, but never that fast," he argued.

"Maybe you got faster," I tried, not really sure what he meant. "And what's a first life?"

"We count lives," he began. "When you're born, you start your first life, which lasts until the first time you die. When you wake up, that's the start of your second life, and so on until one day you don't wake up anymore," he explained. At least he, Embry and Gabriel were all consistent in their story.

"I'm...I guess that puts me in my second life," I admitted.

"That explains it, then," he said, but there was a sadness to him now. He was beginning to see me as a flawed and broken freak instead of the sweet and vulnerable human he thought I was.

"It doesn't explain anything," I argued.

"I was stabbed and now I'm fine," he pointed out.

"So was I," I admitted. "That's what made everyone think I was Gifted in the first place. If you already know you're Gifted, then that's what happened."

"It normally takes longer, and you die first. I was conscious the whole time."

"The whole time?" I asked.

"I drifted a bit when we were in the alley, but I started feeling better almost as soon as you touched me, and I felt this heat all over my body. It was weird, almost like your heat was healing my wounds."

"That doesn't make any sense," I argued, mostly trying to remember what I said to him on the ride over.

"None of this makes sense," he shrugged, but he had this smile, like some kind of weight had been lifted. "Coming back to life no matter what happens to us, random abilities..."

"What do you have?" I asked.

"Superhuman strength," he said like it was obvious.

"Don't you just get that from...you know, naturally?"

He laughed at me, with the smile reaching his eyes. "Yes, I do get a lot of it naturally, but I could never lift enough weights to do this," he explained, punching a tree behind him. The trunk was at least twice as wide as I was, but it snapped like a twig. Caleb's reflexes were also faster than mine, because he caught the falling top of the tree before I even brought my hands up over my head. "Your friend can use this for firewood," he suggested, holding the tree like it weighed less than a single branch.

"That's..."

"Impressive?" he finished for me.

"I was going to say terrifying," I argued, but I was smiling. For a second, it was like it didn't matter that nothing made sense anymore, because I wasn't alone in the crazy. And then I heard the sirens.

"There he is!" a man yelled, followed by a rush of men coming close to apprehend Caleb. At the head of them was William.

"I'm sorry," I whispered to Caleb before retreating into the woods. I wasn't sure what was going on, but I knew that I couldn't be seen.

"You are under arrest for the murder of Loretta Crane," William said before tying Caleb's hands behind his back.

CHAPTER SIXTEEN

I rushed back to Cassandra's as soon as the constables were gone, to tell her and Alan what happened.

"He's found a way to get rid of the man who stood in his way and could identify him, then solved your murder in the process."

"But Caleb is innocent, and William belongs behind bars," I pointed out. "We need to get Caleb out of there, as soon as possible."

"I'll go see my lawyer," Alan offered.

"I don't think we have that long," I argued.

"Trials take…"

"William won't wait for a trial. If Caleb talks, he can tell everyone who was really there this morning, and that he wasn't even in town when I was murdered. William's only chance of making this work is to get rid of Caleb before anyone decent can talk to him."

"Then let's get to work," Cassie assured me, taking her coat.

"I can't just walk into the constabulary and tell them they have the wrong person. As you so kindly pointed out, as far as they're concerned, I'm dead. If William sees me, he might murder me all over again."

"You can't, but according to you, there's another woman out there who can," she reminded me.

"Do you know how to find her," I asked, but I followed her just the same.

ALL WE HAD to go on was that she was a teenager with blonde hair, a busted lip, and possibly a limp, but somehow, Cassie was optimistic.

"There are some women who suffer through something like that, go home to their husbands and get the treatment they need. Others keep it all inside because they know they would be blamed for it..."

"How does that help us?" I asked.

"The way you described her, she sounds like the third type; a woman who doesn't have a husband to go home to. If she's on the streets, there's only one place she can go."

CASSANDRA SOUNDED CONFIDENT, so once Mr. Lovell dropped us off, I followed her through the streets of town to a small boarding school.

"Miss Chanterelle's School for Girls?" I asked. It did not sound like a place for women who lived on the street.

"It's expensive to care for all the women who have nothing, so Miss Chanterelle runs an elite boarding school with a very hefty price tag, then uses the profits to run a school for Wayward girls in the back."

"That's incredible."

"She truly is."

"Mrs. Roosevelt!" the little girl who opened the door for us exclaimed.

"Is your mother home?" Cassandra asked her.

"Mama!" she ran off into the building, yelling as she went.

"Come on," Cassandra told me, so I followed her into the foyer and shut the door behind me.

"Cassie?" A woman, I'm guessing Miss Chanterelle, came down a gorgeous staircase. She was so graceful it looked like she was floating.

"Miss Chanterelle," Cassandra acknowledged before they took each other in for a hug.

"How can I help you?"

"We're here because there was a woman who was injured in an altercation with the same men who hurt my friend here, and we were hoping we could talk to her, maybe find out what she saw," Cassie shrugged at the end, completely downplaying the severity of our situation.

"We have very strict policies on that, which you are well aware of."

"Of course, and I would never use any of the information against anyone, but if this woman wanted a chance to put the men who hurt her away, and prevent the man who rescued her from going to jail for it…"

"He survived?" Miss Chanterelle betrayed herself.

"Not for long if we don't help him." Cassie knew she had her.

"I'll ask around, see if anyone heard anything." Miss Chanterelle got up and snapped her fingers for two twelve-year-old girls to bring us tea and an assortment of sweets.

"In my line of work, I encounter a lot of women who need a place to get back on their feet," Cassie explained her connection to the school.

"It's a great thing she's doing," I agreed.

I WAS ALMOST DONE my tea by the time Miss Chanterelle came back with a young woman. Even with her head down and her hair combed, I could tell it was the one from the alley. She still had my shawl.

"Miss," she said to me, doing a tiny bow.

"That's completely unnecessary," I assured her.

"Mary here was walking home from the bakery last night, when—"

"You saved me," she finished for Miss Chanterelle.

"Caleb saved you," I argued.

"It wasn't the first time that they tried...these men own the streets. Mostly at night, but if it's a cloudy or a quiet day...they're not picky," her voice was trembling and she kept her head down, but she didn't stop talking.

"I knew I shouldn't risk it with so few people in the streets, but it was my mother's birthday and I had to get her something," she explained. "One of them came and asked me for directions, but when I turned to point him towards the hospital, I saw the others. I was surrounded and thought it was the end for me, one way or the other. I was resigned to it, until you both came and saved my life, my honor, everything." She looked up for the last sentence, her eyes full of tears.

"Would you be able to recognize these men?" Cassie asked her.

"Of course. I see nothing but his eyes, every time I close mine."

"Would you consider coming to the constabulary with me to tell them the man they've arrested is innocent?"

"My word wouldn't count for anything," she argued.

"It counts for everything." I almost believed Cassie; she said it with such conviction. "As long as someone is brave enough to speak the truth, there will always be someone there to listen."

"Do you live in a fantasy world, or are you just hoping I do?"

"I'm hoping that you'll do what's right, even if it might not work, because Caleb stood between you and a group of drunk and angry men, knowing he might die for it. Which I believe he was fine with, only I couldn't stand to see the man who faced your rapists go down in history as one of them."

"I can make a statement, if you think it will help, but..."

"But what?" I asked when she trailed off.

"One of them was a constable," she explained.

"I know," I assured her.

"We can go when he isn't working. As long as someone hears your statement, the seed of doubt is planted, and we have something to work with."

"And if they decide they don't want me talking?"

"I will leave you with my driver, Mr. Lovell. Whenever you are ready, he will escort you right into the constabulary, and stay with you while you give your statement, if needed."

"I don't know if I can go today," Mary argued.

"It doesn't matter. Go when you're ready. The driver will be waiting."

"And how will you get home?"

"Don't you worry about me," Cassie assured her.

"And Mary?" I asked, stopping her as she went to leave back through the hallway she came from.

"Yes?"

"Thank you. For helping him. I know he's not here to say it now, but I'm sure he truly appreciates this."

"You ladies should be careful," Mary suggested before leaving us.

"Now what?" I asked Cassie.

"Now we wait for her to do the right thing."

CHAPTER SEVENTEEN

That evening, I decided to go to the constabulary. Cassie agreed to let me take her other driver to deter any potential attacks, but I was more afraid of the men inside the building than the ones on the streets. Although they seemed to be one and the same lately.

I made sure not to be seen as I made my way to the window William had shown me ages ago, that led into the holding cell. People from town either used it to give food to the prisoners, or throw scraps at them in a degrading manner, but a hole was a hole.

"Etta?" Caleb was surprised when I showed up and whispered his name.

"I was starving when I first woke up, so I figured you might be," I explained, handing him down a handkerchief filled with cheeses, bread, grapes and a bit of honey.

"Not in the supernatural waking from the dead way, but I haven't eaten in a really long time." He had such an easy smile.

I had intended to bring him the food and then go to work on his case. Instead, I found myself sitting on the eroded cobblestones that could easily give him a way out if he ever did the tiniest bit of digging. Or rather punching.

"It's not much, but I'll come around again tomorrow, and as often as I can."

"You seemed to be avoiding the constabulary earlier," he called me on it.

"Some things are more important," I assured him.

"Are you planning on rescuing me through this hole?" he asked, thinking I was crazy.

"No, but I'll do everything in my power to make it a little more pleasant for you."

"You're off to a good start because your company is the only thing I think might stand a chance."

"We'll get you out of here," I promised.

"You're taking this all with much too much guilt," he warned me.

"How much guilt should I feel for being the reason you almost died?"

"I will never regret helping that woman," he assured me.

"You're truly one of the good ones, Mr. Fletcher," I told him.

"Likewise, Miss Crane."

"How are they treating you?" I asked, even though Alan warned me not to. I was either going to really not like the answer, or Caleb was going to lie to me to spare my feelings.

"Not bad, considering. I don't think they were ever going to feed me or give me anything to keep warm with all of these drafts, but they could be torturing me. Or they could have killed me already. My theory is that it can always be worse, so enjoy the few things that are going right instead of all of the things you need to fix." It was excellent advice, but today I didn't want to think of all the ways it could be worse. I was getting cold, so I pulled the shawl tighter around myself, and huddled closer to the wall, as if I could get some of his heat through the bars.

"We've spoken to the woman you saved. We're hoping she'll testify and tell them you were her rescuer, not an aggressor," I shared.

"You're also assuming they'll listen."

"I have a friend who went to school with my sister. I'm not sure I trust my judgment anymore, but if I had to bet on it, I would say he's a stand-up guy who will find the truth if we show it to him."

"I appreciate it," he told me, but he clearly didn't have much faith in the plan.

"Have you been in jail before?" I asked, noticing how calm and relaxed he was. I would be panicking and banging on the bars for someone to let me out.

"A few times," he said guiltily. "I do my best to avoid trouble, but it has a way of finding me."

"What's the worst thing you've been charged with?" I asked.

"Worst thing I actually did, or just that they accused me of doing?"

"Is there much of a difference?"

"Well, I'm currently in jail for murdering you. And the attempted rape of young women, but I've done neither."

"I guess I always assume the justice system works as it should."

"I thought so too," he agreed. "But my whole life, being tall and wide made people fear me and assume the worst. I normally stay very far away from women who are out on their own at night, because no one finds me reassuring."

"I do," I argued. "Obviously not at first, but once I got to know you…I definitely feel safer when you're around."

"Even with the bars between us?"

"Those are cumbersome," I amended. "Couldn't you just…" I made a motion like I was pulling the bars apart, which got him to laugh.

"If this were a town where no one knew me, I could do that and move on."

"But?" I asked, sensing it had to do with me.

"But I wouldn't want to put your friends in jeopardy, and I'm not so ready to move on."

"The right men need to be put in jail," I agreed.

"That too," he said, staring deep into my eyes, so I felt like he could see right down into my soul, into every part of me; the good, the bad and the ugly. Somehow, for him I didn't mind.

"I should go work on your case," I said, getting up and trying not to show how flustered I was.

"You're a kind woman, Etta. Better than I deserve."

"From the little I know of you, I would say you deserve a lot better," I argued.

CHAPTER EIGHTEEN

When I got back to Cassandra's, she and Alan were talking over whiskey by the fireplace, while her friend Embry was asleep on the sofa.

"Is he okay?" I asked. I took a seat and accepted the glass Alan poured me.

"He will be," she said, rubbing her temple and looking exhausted. "It seems the two of you have a friend in common."

"Embry and I?" I asked, knowing that we both knew her. A chill crossed the back of my neck at the thought of him knowing William, which didn't make sense.

"He came to ask me for help looking for his friend, Caleb, who never made it back to their hotel for dinner," she explained.

"You told him I got his friend arrested?"

"I told him Caleb intervened on a woman's behalf and got falsely accused for it," she removed any blame from me.

"He's a good man," I said. "He's kind and honest and protects the people who need it, whether they want it or not...I keep thinking that if only I had met him before...before William took my life away from me..."

"The way I see it, you're both still here," she pointed out.

"But I can't be me," I argued. "I've been putting off moving to Paris for years, because I was afraid of being on my own and leaving my sister, but now I think maybe it was so I could meet Caleb. I would have been more trusting of a man who approached me on a street corner at night. I would have been touched that he wanted to walk me home. I would have let him call on me and one thing could have led to another and I could have had the life I dreamed of. Now, even if we clear his name, I can't get married in this town, or raise children in it. My kids will never get to know their cousins or be cherished by their aunt. Unless she agrees to move away with us, which I guess she might once she finds out her husband is a murderer…" I was rambling, mostly to myself, but I could tell that something I said disagreed with Cassandra. She was looking at me like something terrible had happened and she didn't know how to tell me. "What's wrong?" I asked.

"It is my understanding that Gifteds can't have children," she said delicately, biting down on her bottom lip.

"What do you mean?" I asked. "You said we come back just as we were."

"You do. Every time, you will come back just as you are now. You won't grow any older…it's like time is suspended for you. But that means you can never get pregnant, and Caleb can never father a child." As she said it, she cradled her own stomach, looking just as devastated as I felt.

"Never?" I asked.

"Not as long as you're Gifted."

It felt like the wind was knocked right out of me. Of course, I knew I should be grateful. It was silly of me to expect anything at all. I died. I was lucky to be back in any capacity…but the fact that I woke up made me think that I was back to being me, that as long as I went somewhere people didn't know I had died, I could still get married and have children like I had always dreamed. I never knew anything about my future, other than that I wanted children.

"You're welcome to stay here as long as you'd like. It's just Alan and I, and he's always gone on business," she said.

I nodded without really listening, staring at the fire but not really seeing it.

"I'll see you upstairs," Alan said, kissing his wife on the forehead before leaving us alone with Embry's occasional snore.

"I'm so sorry," Cassie told me after a few minutes in silence. "I know how hard it is to hear—"

"How?"

"I'm not sure how it all works, Gabriel knows more about the science—"

"How do you know what it feels like? You're still human, aren't you? You're not broken." I said the words to her, but the anger was aimed at myself and the world. Unfortunately, Cassie looked as hurt as if I had slapped her.

"I am human," she agreed. "But I'm also broken. Alan rushed back from his trip because I miscarried again. Or rather had a still-birth. It's happened enough times that I'm well aware of the difference between the two." Her tears fell in huge drops that made my heart, and my womb, ache even more.

"I had no idea. You've been so..."

"Brazen and fearless, burying myself in other things so I don't feel it?" she offered.

"Is that why Embry came?" I asked, realizing that Embry must be Caleb's friend who came to see someone going through a tough time.

"It's why he came earlier than his usual visit, and why Gabriel was so reluctant to leave," she agreed. "It's also why we were at the hospital when you woke up. I made him steal the autopsy report, hoping there would be something to explain why my babies keep dying, but it's just me."

"I'm so sorry," I repeated her words, knowing how little they helped.

"I wasn't sharing for sympathy. Just letting you know I understand, and it doesn't mean you're broken. If you want a family, all you have to do is make one."

I had originally planned on going up to bed before she could see my tears, but instead, we stayed up and finished the bottle of whiskey.

CHAPTER NINETEEN

JANUARY 9TH, 1843

I woke up grateful I remembered to drink water before going to sleep, so the headache was manageable. There was also another dress at the foot of the bed, so I put it on and went downstairs, where Cassandra and Embry were about to have breakfast.

"Tea?" she asked me.

"Tea would be lovely," I agreed, taking a seat. Embry looked defeated, but Cassandra was avoiding eye contact with me. "More bad news?" I asked.

"Mr. Lovell came home right after you went to bed last night," she started. I could tell by the way Embry balled his hands into fists that I was about to discover why he was so upset.

"How is Mary?" I asked, letting her know it was okay to continue with the story, but she just looked guilty.

"When she went to the station, they showed her a portrait of Caleb and told her he was the man who tried to hurt her. When she insisted Caleb was the one who protected her from a group that included a constable, he told her she was misremembering because of the trauma, and they already had enough testimonies. He threatened to hurt her if she didn't go along with it. She told Mr. Lovell she refused, but as they were leaving, he heard the constable tell his captain that she'd identified Caleb."

"But that's not what happened," I argued.

"It doesn't matter what the truth is, it matters what they say it is. With 'the law' on their side, there's nothing Caleb can do or say," Embry explained bitterly.

"How are we going to get him out?" I asked, but I was met with blank stares. "We have to do something," I pressed.

"There's nothing we can do," Cassandra explained. "At least not for Caleb. I've heard they have him on multiple counts, from women who are too afraid to stand up to the constables, or who will say anything for a warm meal and some change. They have witnesses corroborating a constable's story, so there won't be a trial."

"We can't just let him rot in jail. We need to go back to Miss Chanterelle's so we can talk to Mary and—"

"He wasn't sentenced to jail," Embry told me.

"No," I argued. I'd mentioned it as an outcome we had to prevent, but I never thought we would actually get there.

"They're executing him this afternoon."

"I am not sitting back and letting William do what he did to me to another woman while he is still married to my sister, raising my niece and nephew." I pictured Billy, so sweet and innocent. I could not let him turn into his father.

"We won't, Lorie. I don't know how, but we will stop him. I promise you."

I nodded, but I was beginning to think there was nothing we could do.

CHAPTER TWENTY

I t was the coldest day yet, but the streets were so crowded that I didn't even feel the chill. Cassandra offered to come for support, but Alan reminded her of their appointment with an obstetrician, so they left not long before Embry and I got into the carriage together.

"So, you're Etta," he stated.

"Only Caleb calls me that," I argued, wondering if he'd visited him since the arrest, or if Caleb had mentioned me to him before.

"He mentioned as much," he shared like he knew some secret I wasn't privy to. "I haven't seen him that happy, where even his eyes are smiling, in…I don't think I've ever seen it."

"This town agrees with him," I suggested, realizing he was probably going to hate anything even remotely related to this town after tonight.

"I think you do," Embry argued.

I gave him a sad smile, then we spent the rest of the ride staring out in silence.

"It's over here," Embry told me once we got out.

"Have you been to many of these?" I asked, following him.

"More than I care to remember," he sighed, and for the first time, I could believe that he was hundreds of years old. His skin and face looked as young as ever, but his eyes looked like he'd seen centuries of loss and heartache.

"Were you ever in his shoes?"

"Once," he agreed.

"Does it hurt?" I asked, knowing I shouldn't, but I wanted to know.

"Not as much as watching," he found us a spot close enough to the platform that Caleb would be able to find us in the crowd, but far enough that we could make a quick exit, and escape if it was too much for me.

"I find that hard to believe."

"There was a little fear, and a bit of pain, but ultimately it was over within minutes and I woke up as if nothing had happened," he said of his own hanging. "But I still have nightmares of watching the flames take someone I love. That's what haunts me centuries later," he explained.

"I didn't think of that," I realized, knowing that the fact that Caleb would probably wake up didn't give much comfort at the moment. "Were they also—"

"She wasn't Gifted," he cut me off.

"I'm so sorry," I said. The words wouldn't help, but I meant them with every fiber of my being. I had never been to a public hanging. Georgina and I usually stayed home while William went to them, but I couldn't remember hearing of one where a woman was convicted. I wanted to ask what crime sent her to the gallows, but his eyes told me the centuries had done absolutely nothing to dull the pain, and I wasn't going to be the one to make him relive it.

It looked like the entire constabulary had gathered on the platform, but William was the one who went up to speak.

"As you all know, a few nights ago, my sister-in-law, the beautiful, kind-hearted Loretta Crane, was murdered in these here streets, stabbed and discarded like an animal. I vowed to find the man responsible for causing so much pain, not just to my little sister, but to my wife, and to our two children, who keep asking me when Aunt Lorie is coming home," he paused and bowed his head, as if overcome by emotion, making me want to puke. Embry knowingly took my hand in his and gave it a squeeze, reminding me that I was safe, and we would make sure he paid for his crimes.

"Two days ago," William continued, "Mary Martin was walking home to her mother when the same monster who preyed on my sister tried to attack her, right in the middle of Baker street, where we let our children play, believing them to be safe."

I shook my head at his ability to lie so convincingly. I guess if he was lying about who did the attacking and how torn up he was about it, he might as well lie about where he lets his children play. I was warned, the first time I took little Billy out in a pram without Georgina, that I was to avoid Baker Street at all costs, unless I was properly accompanied, because only prostitutes and scum frequented that street. Now I knew he was that scum he warned me about.

"Luckily for Mary, a few men happened to be walking by at that very moment, and scared Mr. Fletcher away, letting Mary escape. We apprehended him arguing with another unidentified female in the woods. She understandably fled when we showed up, terrified of what this monster was going to do to her."

My hand that wasn't being held by Embry balled into a fist so tight I could feel my fingernails digging into my skin.

"Today, it is my great honor to carry out Caleb Fletcher's sentence of death by hanging, so he will never be able to prey on our good women again."

The crowd, understanding that he was done talking, erupted into applause that quickly turned into a chant of "Let him hang! Let him hang!" that made me sick.

"Are you sure you want to stay?" Embry tried to whisper, but it was impossible to hear him over all of the shouting.

"If Caleb looks up, I want to be here," I told him.

"I don't think he would want you to see this," Embry argued.

"I don't think he wants to die alone," I said simply, taking a step forward.

Caleb, who had been brought out for the crowd to see, with his hands tied behind his back, had kept his head down up to this point, but when they brought him to the noose, he finally looked up. He seemed so crushed by the magnitude of people cheering on his death, but it wasn't long until he found Embry and I, standing still in the crowd, trying to send him all of the support in the world. His eyes locked on mine and at first his entire body slumped. I was thinking Embry was right and I shouldn't have come, but then he smiled at me. It was a sad smile, the kind you use when a friend accompanies you to something unpleasant, so you don't have to go through it alone. He didn't want me there, to see him like that, but he was grateful that I was.

"Any last words?" William asked Caleb once the noose was around his neck and he was standing on the trap door.

Caleb glared at William before looking back to Embry and I. "The truth will always win, as long as there are people brave enough to share it," he said to the crowd at large.

"The truth already won," William said, but my eyes were on Caleb.

His eyes locked with mine. I wanted to take all of his pain away as they tightened the noose around his neck, but he kept his eyes on me as if he didn't even notice. I could see in my peripheral vision that William made some kind of signal with his arms, but I still screamed when they released the trap door.

I was grateful for Embry's hand holding mine as Caleb fell through. I heard a snap, that I felt deep within my chest, but it took Caleb a few minutes, and some tugging, before they finally called his death.

CHAPTER TWENTY-ONE

I had to look away once Caleb was hanging, but it wasn't like he could see me anymore at that point.

"Let's get you home," Embry decided, trying to bring me back to Cassandra's before the crowd got bored and dispersed.

"Not without Caleb," I argued.

"Cassie has a contact at the morgue, we'll get him back," he assured me.

"I'll wait," I decided, heading off in the direction of the morgue. I knew Caleb was gone now, and wouldn't be back for at least a couple of hours, but I couldn't stand the thought of him being alone.

CASSIE'S CONTACT worked the graveyard shift, so he didn't arrive at the morgue until at least an hour after Caleb's body was carried in. Embry and I hid across the street so we wouldn't be spotted, but as soon as the contact arrived, he ushered us inside.

"Lionel, I believe you've met my friend Lorie," Embry said with a smile. I could see his Gift slowly relaxing the poor man, who did not look happy to see us.

"I was hoping that's what happened to you," he said once we

were in his office, explaining the weird look he'd been giving me. Not that I remembered it, but I had been on his table mere days ago, before I woke up and escaped with Gabriel and Cassandra. It felt like lifetimes now.

"You can have your coat back. I'm sorry I took it, I just didn't have much else to—" I went to remove his coat, that I'd been walking around in since I woke up, but he stopped me.

"No, keep it. I dare say it looks better on you, and my wife got me a new one," Lionel assured me.

He gave us tea while we waited, but still reproached Embry for assuming he would always help out whenever we needed it. Apparently, Lionel had agreed to let Cassie and her friends claim bodies, as long as they walked out on their own. A week ago, I would have thought he was crazy and sent him to a physician, but now it was an arrangement that made perfect sense to me.

Embry suggested I sit in the office while we wait, so I could have a comfortable chair and not be so cold, but I could tell Lionel was nervous I would be discovered, and I didn't want to be that far from Caleb. For some reason, I felt like waking up alone would be worse than dying.

So, I drank my tea and progressively got closer to the room where Caleb's body rested on a metal slab in the center. He definitely looked dead, with his skin a ghostly shade of white, and purple lines around his neck, but I was more than happy to believe the Gifted theory that he would come back to life, just as he had been when I met him.

I had somehow fallen asleep, but woke up when Caleb finally stirred. I was mostly composed by the time he opened his eyes. "Good morning, sleepy head," I said with a smile. It took him a lot less time to come back than I had.

He looked at me with confusion, and for a moment I was terrified that you forgot things when you woke up, but then he smiled. "You haven't been waiting here all night, have you?" he asked.

"Haven't left your side," I assured him.

"I never took you for the morbid type." He shook his head, pretending to be concerned.

"More the kind who thinks people should die surrounded by friendly faces, and wake up to the same," I shared.

"It's a first but it's nice," he said as he stretched, flexing his muscles in the process. I hid the smile, but there was nothing I could do for the blushing.

"How do you usually wake up?" I asked, mostly to distract him from my face, but also to find out if there was, or ever had been a Mrs. Fletcher.

"Alone," he said simply, but there was a vulnerability in the way his eyes met mine. "Or surrounded by very confused bystanders, and terrified morticians," he brought us back to joking.

"I imagine you've caused a few fainting spells," I played along.

"None worth noting," he said it reassuringly, as if he didn't want me to worry. "And a lot less than you're imagining," his smile faded. "It didn't seem fair to pursue anyone when I can't stick around."

"You do look rather young." I felt that was the easiest thread to expand on without revealing myself.

"Twenty-One," he agreed.

"Same as me," I said nervously, realizing that I would never get any older. "How did you... I mean, if it's not too..."

"I was fighting in the Texas revolution," he reiterated, stopping my flubbing. "My brother enlisted, and I usually did whatever he did. We were young and stupid and thought we were invincible. He got shot in the leg, but he told me to give them hell for him, so I went out, without my brother-sized-superstitious armor, and got shot. Lots of times. At first, with the adrenaline, it kind of felt like a bee sting, but then everything happened so fast. It got really cold, and everything around me was spinning, until it all went black."

"Was Embry fighting with you?" I asked.

"No, he was travelling through, Lord knows why. The other side was collecting their dead and confirming their kills, but Embry heard two of them talking about a soldier who rose from the dead."

"What did they do with you?" I asked. There was something in his eyes that told me it wasn't as simple as Embry walking over and them becoming travel buddies.

"Turns out I was one of the bodies they'd already stabbed with a bayonet, so they stabbed me again and got the hell away from me."

"I'm so sorry." I was horrified.

"You didn't do it," he assured me.

"I'm sorry that happened to you. I'm sorry I asked. And I'm sorry I got you killed this afternoon."

"I would do it all again in a heartbeat." He locked eyes with me. "The getting hanged for protecting a woman and avenging your death part. Getting shot, then stabbed, then waking up alone with a bunch of dead bodies is something I would be fine with not repeating."

"I have the feeling I can't do much about you defending the helpless, but as long as I can help it, I won't let you do it alone," I swallowed, terrified that I'd overstepped, but also afraid of what would happen if I let him walk away without saying it.

"The dying or the waking up?" he asked, not turned off in the least.

"All of it," I said, my voice shaking.

"We can start with your brother-in-law," he said, brushing my hair away from my face. Only then did I remember that I had fallen asleep and must look a mess.

"He needs to be gone from that house, somewhere he can never get close to my sister, his children, or any women in general." The anger welled up in me.

"Ready to walk out now?" Embry poked his head in. "I heard voices."

"Let's get this asshole," Caleb agreed.

CHAPTER TWENTY-TWO

JANUARY 10TH, 1843

Mrs. Lovell had a large meal waiting for us when we returned. I hadn't eaten since lunch the day before, but who knows when Caleb's last meal was. I wasn't surprised when he went for the food as soon as the official introductions were made.

I was about to follow them into the dining room when I saw Cassie's gloves on a table, the white ones she wore the night we met. I hadn't noticed it then, but there were tiny claw-like extensions sticking out, which explained William's scratched face.

"Cassie likes jewelry and dresses, but if I really want to make her happy, I find some kind of harmless object and turn it into a deadly protective weapon for her. These gloves were her wedding present, her shoes are from our first anniversary—"

"What's wrong with her shoes?" I asked, but he just gave me a secretive smile before going to his wife.

Suddenly, I got an idea. I quickly stuffed the gloves into my coat pocket before anyone could notice, and headed for the door.

"Where are you going?" Caleb asked, poking his head out from the dining when he noticed I wasn't joining them.

"I didn't get much sleep, so I'm just going to get in a few hours before we get to work." I felt bad for lying to him, but this wasn't something anyone else could do in my place. It had to be me.

"Sweet dreams," he gave me an apologetic smile, knowing he was the reason I didn't sleep, then he went back to the others.

I WAS GOING TO WALK, but Mr. Lovell insisted on bringing me. This had been going on long enough, and it wasn't like he could make it back and tell on me before I accomplished my task. Or died trying. Again.

I HAD Mr. Lovell bring me to Simon's office first, so I could leave him a note with the gloves. As long as Simon got to town before the scratches on William's face disappeared, it should provide him with the necessary proof to put William away. Next, I asked Mr. Lovell to bring me home.

I OPENED the gate and paused, looking up to the house that was my home, but now felt foreign. I completely understood what Caleb meant, and it broke my heart. I took a deep breath, peering into the windows on my way to the front door, but they must be upstairs, or eating in the dining room.

"Can I help you?" a new maid asked, opening the door.

"Is Georgina home?" I asked, swallowing against my nerves, not that it helped.

"Who might I say is calling?"

"A friend," I said, hoping it would be enough.

The girl looked me up and down, trying to decide if I was a threat or not, but ultimately decided I wasn't going to hurt anyone.

"Wait here while I go fetch her," she told me.

· · ·

My plan was to tell my sister what William did to me, knowing it would crush her, terrified that she wouldn't believe me, but knowing that I had to do it in order to protect her. I didn't plan on seeing anyone else, or addressing the fact that I was dead, yet standing right in front of her, because I had no satisfying way to explain it.

Unfortunately, almost as soon as I was left alone, Catherine waltzed in, wearing the fairy wings I'd sewn for her, that I was supposed to mend after Billy's dragon tore them, but never got around to.

"Auntie Lorie?" she asked me, confused for a second before she ran straight into my arms.

I was holding her close, feeling like my heart was in pieces, and put back together at the same time, when I heard the footsteps of Mrs. Wells, our cook. "Miss Catherine!" she exclaimed, and knew I was in trouble. "Miss Loretta," she added, shocked when her eyes landed on me.

"Lorie?" Georgina nearly fainted when she came up behind Mrs. Wells. She looked torn between rushing into my arms as well, or ripping her child away from me.

"Why don't you go see mummy?" I told my niece, my heart breaking as I let her go, especially when I saw how my sister was looking at me. "Can we talk?" I asked her.

"William said…"

"I know."

"He had my shawl."

"I can explain."

"Why don't I go make everyone some tea," Mrs. Wells took Catherine into the kitchen, leaving me alone with my sister.

"He said you died," Georgie managed to get the words out.

"I did," I agreed.

"That makes no sense," she argued.

"What comes next makes even less sense," I told her.

"Maybe we should wait for him to come home," she tried. I could see how much she hated it, but she was afraid of me.

"That's not a good idea," I warned.

"Lorie...I want to take you into my arms and never let you go, but you're not making it easy," she warned.

"Didn't you always tell mother I made everything harder?"

"What happened to you?"

"Bruno wasn't in the yard, but a man found me looking for him and offered to help. He said he'd seen a dog in the alley and..."

"He hurt you..." she was angry, and shocked.

"He tried to rape me," I continued the story. "He forced himself on me, and I couldn't stop him..."

"Who did this to you?" she bridged the distance and tried to take me in her arms, but I had to finish telling her.

"I threatened to tell you. That was the thing that stopped him, but he realized that I was going to tell you whether he finished or not, so he stabbed me. A woman showed up and stopped him, but I was bleeding so much that she couldn't save me, and I died."

"You can't have, Lorie, you're standing in front of me."

"I can't explain that part, but—"

"Why would telling me stop him?" she asked, catching on.

"The man was William," I admitted.

"He didn't see you that night," she argued.

"He did. He did a lot more than just see me."

"*My* William tried to hurt you?"

"He didn't try Georgie, he hurt me. More than I have ever been hurt before. And I can't explain it. Even while it was happening, I thought I must be wrong. I woke up after dying and him doing that was still the most confusing part of my night."

"You have to be confused, Lorie, he would never do that to you. He loves you like I do; like a sister. We need to get you help," she tried to take me in her arms again, but I put my hands out to stop her.

"He broke my heart too, Georgie, but you're the one who needs help." I took a deep breath. "The woman who saved me had these gloves with sharp ends, almost like claws..." I paused to let it sink in, as she made the connection to the scratches on her husband's face.

She looked at me, at first like she didn't understand, but then like she did.

"I'll kill him," she said, tears pouring down her face, but there was no pain, only conviction.

"You're not the first to make that offer, but that won't solve this. He has friends and they need to be stopped," I told her.

"With my bare hands, I will…" she looked at me with such guilt and horror, that I took her in my arms, comforting her after a lifetime of the contrary.

"You need to go upstairs and get some things for you and the children. We need to get you away from him."

She was about to argue and say he wouldn't hurt her, but then she looked at me and knew that he already had.

"Billy is in the yard, could you…"

"Of course," I assured her, hoping he would have the same reaction as his sister to seeing me back from the dead.

CHAPTER TWENTY-THREE

I didn't see Billy right away, but I knew exactly where I would find him. We had hollow bushes that he treated like his own private fort. It gave me quite the heart attack the first time he disappeared into it.

I was maybe a hundred feet from the bushes when I heard men in the stables. I imagined they were drunk, because they were singing very loudly and off-key, slurring their words. My first thought was to hide in the bushes with Billy, or run off before he saw me so I could come get Georgie later, but I couldn't leave them with a monster, now that she knew what he was.

"She's up at the house, so be quiet," William probably thought he was whispering, but they were causing a ruckus.

"How long until you can have her again?" a voice I didn't recognize asked.

"Why? You want the others?"

"You shared better before," Murphy agreed.

My legs had carried me to just outside the door, where they shouldn't notice me unless they were really looking for me. Luckily, they were much too concentrated on the alcohol.

"It's a shame about Lorie. She was always so quiet that you just knew she was a devil in the sheets," Felix shared an opinion of me he never even hinted at while I was alive.

"I told you we don't talk about her," William warned.

My first instinct was to be terrified of him, until I remembered that he couldn't hurt me. Well, he could, but no matter what he did to me, I would wake up in the morning and I could haunt him all over again. Because as far as he was concerned, I was dead. He'd even hung the man he claimed was responsible.

"No, please, let me know what you really thought of me." I made a split-second decision, stepping into the middle of the doorway, trying to appear confident and composed.

"Jesus, Mary and Joseph," Felix said before running for the other door, followed by Murphy.

"Lorie," William said, surprised, but there was also a hint of regret and loss that nearly made me lose my nerve.

"Surprised to see me?" I asked.

"Boss, I thought you said...only she doesn't look dead." The man I didn't know was about my height and shaking.

"I'm surprised you told your friends about me. I thought you pinned it all on the man who tried to stop you from raping another woman."

"You can't be here, I...you...."

"You killed me," I agreed, walking towards them like we were talking about something trivial, rather than the biggest betrayal of my existence.

"It was a mistake. I didn't mean to," William said apologetically, making the anger rise up inside me.

"No, you only meant to rape me in a dark alley while your pregnant wife, my sister, slept alone at home with your two children. And it wasn't the first time, was it?"

"I never laid a hand on either of you. I loved you like a sister," he said, and part of me believed him.

"But you were the rapist you stayed out so many nights trying to catch, weren't you?"

"It's not like that. Those women—"

"What changed?" I cut off his excuses. "What made me no longer be your *beloved* sister?" I said 'beloved' sarcastically, but the words stung.

"I was drunk and frustrated. Georgina was all about the baby, but you were wearing her green—"

"That's all it took?"

"I'm sorry."

"Not as sorry as you're going to be."

William flinched at the threat, probably assuming I had some destructive powers I could take my revenge on him with. Instead, I was about to explain to him about the gloves I sent to Simon Davenport, and how Georgina knew the truth, but before I could tell him, my sister walked in with Simon. He was holding Cassie's weaponized gloves and looking at my brother-in-law with disgust.

"I believe I've heard enough." Simon approached William, while Georgina rushed to take me in her arms. I was so relieved that they heard, because there was no way William could deny his involvement after a full confession. Unfortunately, this meant Simon was also looking at me like he was trying to understand how I was standing in front of him if I was dead. I opened my mouth to explain it to him, but I didn't really have an answer that made sense. Simon gave me a nod and a small smile, as if to reassure me we could talk about it later, but I definitely wasn't off the hook.

"Caleb?" I was shocked when he came in and stood behind Simon, as if he were his backup.

"No, this is Daniel, his brother. He seemed to be under the impression that Caleb was preventing an attack, not causing one. I came here to talk to William, but I ran into Mr. Fletcher, and we both encountered William's friends running for their lives."

"They're in your carriage, and the constables have arrived," Caleb assured Simon.

"Thank you, Mr. Fletcher. I am terribly sorry for your brother, and grateful you were here today. If you wouldn't mind," Simon motioned to William once the constables found us.

"Georgie, you can't…it's me. You can't let them…"

William pleaded, but my sister positioned herself as if to shield me from him. "I could murder you right now," she warned.

"I'm your husband," William argued.

"I don't know who you are," she said before bringing me away from him.

CHAPTER TWENTY-FOUR

Mrs. Wells came out with Catherine, while I went into the bushes and found Billy with his hands covering his ears. "It's okay, you're safe now," I told him.

"Auntie Lorie?" he looked at me in amazement before crawling out and wrapping his arms around my skirts.

WE WENT INSIDE where Mrs. Wells had put on tea, but we waited until the children fell asleep from the excitement of the day before we talked. I told Georgie everything about my adventures since I went out looking for Bruno, who was currently asleep under the table.

"I knew I believed you, but I also…it wasn't real until he said it," she shared apologetically, telling me that I wasn't entirely wrong to wait until I had proof before approaching her.

"I still don't believe it," I let her know I felt the same.

"Did you write to Simon?" she asked.

"I knew I could trust him to get to the bottom of it," I shared.

"He got back to town this morning, and rushed over as soon as he read the letter to make sure we were okay."

"What did you tell him about me?" I asked, realizing this complicated things, as I was technically dead.

"We didn't have time to talk about it after he asked me where William was. I couldn't risk him…"

"You don't have to worry about me," I assured her, before explaining about the Gifted. Although maybe my purpose was getting rid of William, so my family would be safe.

"Miss Loretta," the new maid came and waited in the doorway. She looked a lot more cautious now that someone must have told her about my death.

"I won't let them take you. I'll talk to Simon," Georgie assured me, having completely accepted that I was back to life, and decided that things would just go back to the way they were.

"She has a visitor," the lady explained. "A rather large visitor who looks very concerned."

"Mr. Daniel Fletcher," Georgina guessed. "Or rather Caleb?" she tried a little too hard to make it seem like everything was back to normal, but she was genuinely excited when she saw how much I smiled when I talked about him.

"I'll be right out," I assured the maid, trying to fix my hair before following her.

"I see you came home," Caleb said with a sad smile when he saw me.

"This isn't home anymore," I argued. "Too many memories. And Simon might listen to anything my sister tells him for now, but there were people who saw me dead and mourned for me. I can't stay."

"When Cassie couldn't find her gloves, I figured you were either confronting him, or saving your sister, so I came here. I spotted Mr. Davenport just before a man ran straight into me."

"Today's the first time he's ever been good with timing," I sighed.

"Due to some confusion over your current status, they couldn't charge him with your murder, but they have him on over eight counts of rape, and for wrongfully sentencing my 'brother' to death."

"That was some quick thinking," I pointed out.

"People used to confuse us all the time, so when your friend recognized me, I pretended I was my brother."

"What should I call you?" I asked.

"I'm not staying," he said gently. "The whole town watched me die, accused of murder and rape."

"Oh." I tried not to show how hurt I was.

"However," he sounded nervous as he looked down at his feet. "If you were interested, I thought I might spend some time in Europe. Maybe visit France. And, I heard you were an expert on everything Parisian."

"I've never actually been," I argued.

"But you speak French," he pointed out.

"I do," I agreed.

"See, what more do you need?" he gave me a nervous smile.

"Would I be there as your tour guide, or..."

"You could..." he acknowledged the idea. "I thought going together would be easier for you than travelling on your own, and it could just be for the protection...but the truth is that you are the most magnetic woman I have ever met, and I don't want to leave you. Ever. But I don't want to scare you, so I would also be willing to just be your travel companion, to get you to Paris so you can see all the places you dreamed of."

"And if I wasn't afraid?" I asked, slightly holding my breath. He made me feel safe and loved in a way that I had never felt before. It was the thought of him leaving that terrified me.

"Then I was hoping you might consider coming as my wife." He was looking at his feet when he started, but he looked up to me at the end, all hopeful and nervous, making me fall in love with him even more. "I would want you to be my partner. In life and in crime, in anything and everything."

"I would love nothing more," I told him, the smile spreading without my having any control over it.

"Forever for us is a very long time," he warned. "So if you—"

"I want forever," I assured him, stopping his reply with a kiss.

EPILOGUE

SUMMER 1843

The uncertainty about my death – after a dozen people had seen me confronting William – meant that I probably could have chanced a church wedding in town, but Caleb was still in people's minds as the one who committed William's crimes. To be honest, I also hadn't returned to church since I died, because I wasn't ready for the heartbreak that would come if I was denied entry. Instead, we settled for a simple ceremony on the private beach behind Cassandra's house. Rather, it started simple, then evolved into the most elegant and beautiful event I had ever attended in my life.

I ASKED Simon to walk me down the aisle, feeling confident that this brother-in-law would be nothing like the last. Not that anything official had happened yet, but he was at the house every day to check in on them, and on the very short list of people who made my sister smile, no matter what else was going on.

"Last chance to change your mind," Caleb offered when I reached him under the arch at the end of the aisle. He agreed to wait for Paris until Georgina had the baby, so we had a few months hiding out in Cassandra's guest house, to figure out if this was truly what we wanted.

"Absolutely not," I assured him before taking his hand. If anything, I wanted to marry him more now than I did when he first asked. Every new thing I learnt about him made me fall harder. Especially watching him with Billy and Catherine, who adored him almost as much as I did. Georgina's newest, Loretta, wasn't really impressed by anyone yet, but if she was anything like her namesake, she would also be crazy about him.

MRS. LOVELL PREPARED a feast fit for kings, which meant we had to digest a bit before the dancing could really get started. I quickly understood that Gabriel and Embry did not like each other, even if they were both incredibly nice to me. Still, neither of them could refuse when Catherine dragged them onto the dancefloor for the last song before Georgie brought the children home to bed.

WHEN IT GOT DARK, the young woman who came with Delia and Gabriel bewitched at least a couple hundred fireflies to join the party, ensuring we could still find our way. It made everything look as magical as it felt.

Cassandra was taking it easy with the dancing, and slightly avoiding me. She spared no expense for today, but we hadn't really talked in weeks.

"My pain doesn't mean I'm not absolutely thrilled for you," I said, taking my seat at her empty table.

"What do you mean?" she asked, but her hands subconsciously found her stomach.

"You deserve to be a mother," I told her.

"I can't go through it again." I could see that the guilt over her possible happiness was only a tiny part of why she hadn't told me about her pregnancy. She looked terrified.

97

"I have a good feeling about this one." I meant it, but I really had no idea what else to say.

"Me too," she agreed, still afraid, but slowly smiling. "I feel like she's a girl." I'd gone to more meetings for women's rights than I could count in the past few months. I'd always been told I should want a son, to carry on my husband's line, but I could only imagine what a daughter of Cassie's would become.

"I'll bring her something pretty from Paris," I decided.

Cassie looked like she wanted to warn me not to, either out of guilt or fear, but I wasn't having it.

"You were right," I told her. "We can make our own family. Caleb is my home and I have all of you now."

"Always," she assured me.

THE SUN WAS COMING up by the time the party ended, so Mr. Lovell brought us straight to the docks so we could board our ship. I was finally going to see Paris, and I was excited, I truly was. But I was also excited for anything with Caleb. Visiting new places, helping people, building a home together...every aspect of the rest of our lives gave me butterflies.

"Are you ready for an adventure, Mrs. Fletcher?" Caleb asked, lifting me up in his arms to carry me onto the ship. I expected him to put me down once we were on board, but he continued all the way to our cabin, so he could carry me over the threshold.

"I'm ready for anything with you," I said, looking into his dark eyes, which I now knew matched my own. Billy was under the impression I forgot to turn the lights on inside them, but Gabriel explained that the more times a Gifted dies, the darker their eyes become.

"Allons-y, mon amour," he said, showing me the French he'd been practicing for the trip.

"Allons-y," I agreed. I had no idea what our future held, or what my purpose was, but with Caleb, I felt like I was ready for anything.

~

The Gifted stories continue in First Life, Book One of the Gifted Chronicles.

ACKNOWLEDGMENTS

I want to thank my mom for everything she does for the people she loves. She is selfless, caring, and the kind of person I aspire to be. She also went through multiple rereads, and plot adjustments for me.

A huge thank you to Rikki for keeping me in check. Both of you read these books in genres you don't like because you love me, and I appreciate more than I could ever express.

I could not do this without you ladies.

Thank You!

ABOUT THE AUTHOR

Amanda Lynn Petrin grew up on the South Shore of Montreal with a big and supportive family. She studied Psychology and History at McGill University, then went into acting once she graduated. In 2017 she moved to Toronto, Ontario, in the hopes of finding more opportunities. Instead, she discovered that you need to create your own. She has written, produced and starred in multiple short films, including Get-Together, All the Things, Little Bird and Touched. Being an author was a dream she thought would never come true until she started doing the things that scare her. Her debut novel, Shards of Glass, was released in August 2019, and she is just getting started.

Find her at: https://www.amandalynnpetrin.com

ALSO BY AMANDA LYNN PETRIN

Shards of Glass

The Owens Chronicles

Prophecy (Book One)

Destiny (Book Two)

Legacy (Book Three)

Etta: A Gifted Chronicles Novella

The Gifted Chronicles

First Life

Second Chance

Third Eye